RAVE

Rainald Goetz, born in 1954 in Munich, studied History and Medicine in Munich and obtained a doctoral degree in both subjects. He briefly worked as a doctor, but quit this profession for the sake of literature in his early thirties. His first novel, *Insane*, was published in 1983. In 1998, Goetz wrote the internet diary 'Rubbish for Everyone', probably the first literary blog in Germany, with entries on the world of media and consumerism. It was published in book form in 1999 and together with *Rave*, *Jeff Koons*, *Celebration* and *Deconspiration* belongs to *This Morning*, his great history of the present. Goetz has been awarded numerous prizes, most notably the Georg Büchner Prize in 2015. He lives in Berlin.

Adrian Nathan West is the author of *The Aesthetics of Degradation* and translator of such authors as Pere Gimferrer, Juan Benet, Marianne Fritz, and Josef Winkler. His writings appear regularly in the *Times Literary Supplement*, *Los Angeles Review of Books*, the *Literary Review*, and many other publications.

'Goetz's writing is a kind of dancing. Each sentence, fragment, captures the essence of what it's like to live inside the spaces of techno music. Thoughts come and go, and return louder, later in the text, with an urgent rhythm that makes the cumulative case for the transformative power of the dance floor. This is writing of and from the body, hot, sweaty, dazed, decadent, and ultimately life-affirming.'
— Julia Bell, author of *The Dark Light*

'To sample an old saying: if you can remember the nineties, you weren't there. Rainald Goetz was there, and found a form in which to summon the sensations and sounds, the highs and the bass, of techno culture. This is a classic cut from a fabled era that will enrich the mix of today's rave culture – and fills in the memory hole for some of us old-timers'
— McKenzie Wark, author of *The Beach Beneath the Street*

'*Rave* matches [Bernhard] with its pitch-black humour and philosophical intensity. Questions of interiority, the external world, language and meaning are opened up within its circuit of pills and beats and clubs, like a genuinely meaningful drug trip.'
— *Financial Times*

'Spilling out and trying to contain, understanding and rejecting the offered narratives – this is all part of a push and pull we use to learn about the self. It's in this madness, and not aside from it, that Goetz thrives.'
— *BOMB*

'This time it's not blood dripping on his text, but the nocturnal sweat of the techno dancer. Goetz's great achievement is, above all, to have translated the thudding rhythm of this new music into rhythmic language'
— *Frankfurter Allgemeine Zeitung*

Fitzcarraldo Editions

RAVE

RAINALD GOETZ

Translated by
ADRIAN NATHAN WEST

BAM BAM BAM

Westbam

I

COLLAPSE

'The collapse begins.'

... and came up to me in slow motion. I looked, longed, walked, and thought.

I had a feeling of lightness.

Maybe I could make a decision.

'The driver's licence is gone now, now I'll write the book fast.'

Wirr: there I was standing in the middle of the music. – Thrust.

Right away Laarman had secured the film rights for the Schütte saga for some fantastical sum. The money was gone, the accounts closed, the cards cancelled.

I saw him, how he stood there with a young woman behind the pillar, and suddenly he looked to me like a giant. He talked with her, talked past her: really they were talking over one another. Everything friendly, warm, roused.

My face was soaking wet already too.

We went to the other room in the back.

SWEET CONFUSION

You've got to imagine so-and-so as a happy person.

Who was that again?

We looked around and laughed. Dope music now.

'Hey! Look!'

I had the sixteenth notes popping superlight in my fingertips, arms thrown out wide. Them too, teeny tiny glittering forward, up, down, cool.

The glistening jewellery shimmered silver.

Schütte to Wirr: 'Where?'

When a person said the toilets, they didn't necessarily mean somewhere else. The searcher was calm, even when speaking, interpreter in the wordlessness of faces or gazes. The searcher is there, searching for signs.

Who's taking what?

Who's still got some?

Who can still make something happen?

Who's there?

It was the time of the linden blossoms.

Then Mark heard someone close by say the words: 'The state prosecutor is now investigating on suspicion of breach of confidentiality.'

And right away I thought: 'Fantastic.'

And I had Albert's truth-testaments, his drawings, I mean, which were a visible manifestation, from oblique angles, of the collision of temporal planes.

Pausing and pounding.

Then I saw how she –

And turned –

And new glances all round. I laughed, because –

I don't exactly know –

And turned. 'What's up.'

Ah, right, sure. Cool.

OK.

Behind, above, around: enormous now, the supremacies of sound had risen up, giant machines, bigger than a person, that shot thunder through to his insides. He 'looked up, nodded, and felt like an idea borne of the boom-boom-boom of the beat. And the immense boom-boom said: one one one –

and one and one and –

one one one –

and –

cool cool cool cool cool...

He saw Hardy and Leksie, faces and eyes, hurtled, scrambled, shoved, shaken in the midst of the rhythm. Saw broken and blessed, trusting and tender, myriad signs, quick, terse, plain, each blotted out by the next in waves of sympathy. He looked and danced and saw beauty.

From the margins came legs and light, feet, flashes, paces and bass, surfaces and murmurs, equivalencies and functions of a higher mathematics.

He himself was the music.

Then there was a quick cascade of steps, almost tumbling, somehow, from within the rhythms and sounds.

A cascade of nouns,

pertaining to the curtailment and velocity of thoughts correlated to music, with that feeling of contrary facets in aggregate, with the total mental perspective in this moment of simultaneity and the solace of the automaticity of internal processes.

In this direction there would –

A sort of equipoise of contradictions, which without –

And overwrought –

So time, processes, remained intact then. And the conceptual union of opposites: like how before the creation of the world, the so-called spirit of God...

But that, alas, is unthinkable.

And he saw that it was good.

CALLIGRAPHY

When the music, once more for Wirr distinct from –. Not at all. It's just all of a sudden I was thinking: What was that, then? I recognize that. What is that blazing track?

So clear, as though I'd just woken up. For a moment, I found that odd.

I was standing on the dance floor barely moving. Amid the music, I felt a clear connection between hearing and the body that led me automatically inwards, down into the depths. In that instant everything had been foreseen.

Strangely, the back door was closed. Following the lights led again to the floor.

I walked, I stood.

I saw Fabian's face, inquisitive, irritated, maybe.

I gestured, responsive, self-interrogating.

Open situation, new people, T-shirts with text.

I stooped, flicked the lighter.

'Got the time?'

Wirr: at the same time, the question of where I am now in dosage-technical terms.

And I thought: 'Look for Sigi'

We walked down below the DJ. Feelings of gratitude danced before me.

All the years –

This argumentation with records –

Felix nodded at me, elated.

I forgot how to talk
  how to walk and speak
  and I am toward
  flying into the air
  raving

'Techno and hardcore bear the burden of the luminous years of '91 and '92.' Quote.

We would talk about that later, but not now. We were talking about sentences and things.

All that still to come.

Wild feeling.

I thought a moment about Maxim Biller's hate-columns. Then about Diedrich's *War and Peace* in *Spex* way back when. Some kind of breakdown-mechanism brought every *back in the day* to mind, it seemed loathsome, horrible, and tragic, somehow.

And the *back in the day* always vanished every time the bass hit.

'Bass,' I said to Sigi, 'bass, bass, bass.'

The Schütte saga could start that way too, with the boom of bass from afar, through the walls, before the party, with bass, with promise: the party's starting now, big-time.

ENTER THE ARENA

Amid the thudding bass Wirr heard all the bass he'd ever heard in all the life he'd lived up to now, party-panic, break. Then the bass was gone.

No bass.

The bass is gone.

The cessation of the titanic bass, a shoving, a waiting, a holding of breath. Is this some kind of birth canal?

And when the bass dropped back into the beat, a thousand-throated scream rose up.

The people shouted: 'Killer!'

The bass is back.

And they danced and jumped like savages, and a massive monstrous voice said: 'ENTER THE ARENA.'

Enter the arena.

Yeah, cool, definitely, thanks.

Thanks a million.

I'm in. Me too. Me too.

From then on Dark toyed with the idea of reconciling Luhmann's *The Art of Society* with Adorno's posthumous book on Beethoven in his own dissertation on Basic TV.

Dark had short blond hair and was allegedly the personification of something truly evil.

But what was that about?

Harmony lessons, Friday 28.06.1996.

Locus of longing, logos: wordmachine.

Now two dancers with arms flailing high revealed the pale patches of their armpits, and duly the air grew fragrant.

I walked over and danced along. I understood certain secrets about women that one of the two dancers disclosed to me with flippant movements. We looked each other in the eyes and laughed. We danced close to each other; she was wearing a teeny fur. It was easy, light, too. Now and then we touched each other's hands.

I thought about our techno comic. The techno comic atmosphere had to be cool throughout. The plan was a couple of years old now. We wanted to make a film about our lives, partying, music, what things were really like.

But what were things like, really?

I can still see myself sitting there at Wolli's, banging out our lists and ideas one page at a time into the computer – but we always got stuck on two things and couldn't make it any further. And in the end, that was what caused the whole film to flop: the story and the drugs.

There was no story. That was the joke.

Through dancing, I came to think of sexuality.

And then: how once upon a time I wanted to write something about love, maybe a study of Proust, something along those lines, and I would call it Proust Enhanced. If you ask me, Proust's notion of love, however much it is revered, however lofty the style of its execution, is really just as obtuse as the worldview of a little miss editor at *Elle* or *Brigitte*, sorry not sorry.

I let the bass line push me again. It was soft and clear. Then, just like that, it faded away.

Assyrian in wei ge sie te –

And said to Sigi: 'My travels in – '

One time when I was at a Westbam party, that was at the old Halle, outside in Weissensee, maybe even the first May Day –

SEXUALITY

Schütte had ordered a little package from Dark. Now the equipment was set up in the corner, and the camera assistants were there next to it in the dark, up high, nostrils sniffly and flittering.

I walked up to Schmalschleger, who clutched my face in his giant wet hands and kissed my hair. I ought to sniff some out of the other woman's hands, that would be dope.

I was talking with Laarmann and was also taking these gigantic deep draws of breath. And it felt absolutely fantastic. Laarman was talking about the plan for the techno TV thing.

Most people don't have a clue about what kind of guy Laarmann actually is. Laarman snorts and fantasizes and starts rowing his arms. A slightly thinner person can just lean on Laarmann and feel good in his cushiness. And for a second, I did just that.

One time we were sitting on this riverbank in Berlin, in '91 maybe, in front or out back of the old Planet, I think. I still had a crumb of hash left and I rolled a mini-joint, and he and I smoked it together. His girlfriend was there, too. He looked so cute to me, with those blond shocks of hair.

Another time we just sat for four hours in a dark room here in Munich, on the street behind the old patent office. That was dope, too, but not the same way. Mammoth discussions of essential matters, with Kerstin mainly, with Mops. At the end, a few hours where we couldn't say anything more. We sat there, thought a lot, paranoid stuff above all, about the fact of sitting there in such quiet silence, obviously, and no-one said a word. Now and then a question was uttered, to replenish things. Tough stuff, sure.

But cool somehow, too.

Then the woman from before came back from the toilets and the three of us walked to the bar and drank Averna. The woman was chill, the way she moved was crazy chill, laid-back, easy-going. With her sweet little woman's moustache, she was talking to Laarman about basic problems in ethics or logic, anyway that's what I got out of it. Stellar, obviously. Long thick black hair, boyish habitus, funny what with her kinda broad butt stuffed in those low-hanging workers' jeans, cool.

'The happiest moments of my life I have lived in these situations, in these places.'

SLEEP? WHY?

And I saw William opening his arms and shouting:
'Hwill! Hey, Hwill! How's it going?'
'Great! You?'
'Same!'
And I told him about the sentence I'd just thought up.
Him: 'WHAT?'
It was too loud, whatever. We hopped around a bit, one in front of the other, there was a warm feeling, the shared experience of the experience of friendship, then we drifted joyfully apart.

Later she got worried.
They'd already gone on ahead.

Far below, in the shadowy shaft of the riverside, in the roiling and rumbling, peace-making. He lay there asleep.

Desperate wriggling –

A bunch of girls –

I will absolutely do no such thing.

She had seen a friend, a girl, over by the door, totally open, but earlier.

Just that the opportunity never arose.

She didn't know anything about all that.

Maybe just a hint for him –

She'd –

Was he already drunk?

Hardy shouted: 'SLEEPING IS COMMERCE.'

We toasted. Hardy said how he was going to tell all in the Lupo book he was going to write next. He wanted to call this book, which he would think up and write himself, *The Lupo Book*. Everyone laughed, of course they were all into the idea.

Schütte: 'What?'

Wirr thought of the words: 'One of my clients was talking about himself, he said he'd sacrificed his benevolent smile.'

Dark thought of the sentence: 'Every trace of my participation must be erased.'

What held us together was the drugs, to cite Thompson's lawyer Duke. The day after, early morning, the duel.

He was taking care of the soul side of things: quote unquote.

You play the music –

I'll write the book.

Olaf said: 'We were prisoners of the island's drug baron.'

I shouted: 'Yeah!' and laughed.

Then someone said: 'That girl from before was just here again.'

'Really?'

And I said to Hardy: 'So the – '

'Hey!'

'What?'

'Good.'

Max said: 'Good, good, good.'

And repeated that directly: 'Good, good, good.'

Cheer, laughter etc. etc. –

We were in the back again walking to the other bar.

I stood there a while and looked ahead and listened.

I went back.

To the music. Even today, you can't just put this down and say: Yeah, totally cool, I was there... – but increasingly that was the way these thoughts did float up inside me –

And it was –

And I was like –

And it occurred to me, but not urgently, that I was excited to know whether tomorrow I –

etc. etc. –

There was this sentence one morning or one night on Viva or MTV in some pop or rock song from the '80s or

'90s, for some reason I suddenly recalled it, but not why or where I'd got it from, where I wrote it down or why exactly, and so on and so forth.

They were passing a joint, I looked around. I heard something. Wirr was bopping his head. Max was chatting with some big fat foreign guy. Dark had a pack of smokes in his hand. The bass and the brightening lights brought new messages. 'Whatsup?' I turned back. Hardy was talking with Sue, Sue with Cora, Cora motioned to the bar girl, the bar girl nodded. I raised my hand, opened my mouth. The bartender opened the tap, turned her back, bounced on her feet. One of Hardy's homeboys ordered schnapps. Armin came from behind, greetings all round. Where's Schütte? Laarman laughed with a sweeping gesture. William appeared to be in deep agreement with some idea or other. Fabian was standing next to the young woman from last night. She shook her wonderful dark hair.

Then came the continuation.

Which would be like when, unfortunately, a highly sensitive young doctor, impeccably educated, just misses the vein when drawing blood. Then he realizes the nurses can do it. That doesn't cut it.

Every real profession is also a craft. If you can hack it, great. Then it's a pleasure to behold. There is trust, conviction in the extraordinary craftsmanship, the spiritual dimension, the knowledge, the magic of a doctor or DJ.

Pleasant thoughts, cool night.

JUST A QUARTER

Dana said: 'You want a quarter pill, Rainald?'
   I hesitated a second and wavered and uh –
   And thought: 'Er, uh, um hm: why not?'
   And said: 'Nah, thanks, tomorrow I gotta – '
   'Ah, for real, that sucks, right.'
   'Nah, it's totally OK.'
   'Really?'
   We were sitting on the speakers in the back. 'Thirsty.'
We walked to the bar, and Dana held out the quarter pill
for me again. So I took it and held it in my hand between
thumb and forefinger and didn't know whether I'd be
better off sticking it in my mouth or in my pocket.
   'Do whatever you want.'
   If only we knew what it was that we wanted. – Then
we drank some more Averna. Now it felt to me like I was
getting well and proper drunk again.

Pills pills pills
   Girls girls girls
   How did it go again, that tune?

'Helli's standing in the back there,' I said to Caro, 'come
over.' We walked along the edge of the dance floor. It was
tight and dark and extra-packed. The people were leaning in groups and grouplets on the wall. I could feel the
stares of strangers, maybe it was just my imagination.
   To Caro: 'Why are they staring like that?'
   Caro laughed and said: 'Are they? What do you
mean?'
   I laughed too and thought: 'mh mh mh.'

'Herbert,' I said to Hell, 'is going on today with that thing that back in the day Pulsinger used to – '

Before I left, I saw that Hell video *Eat My House* on *House TV* on Viva, I thought that was cool. When was that from? Afterwards we talked about Mike Inc. and Richie Hawtwin.

Richie Hawtwin: dipshit.

Mike Inc.: cheapskate.

'What you got on your nose?'

'Huh?'

'Eh.'

'I mean, it must be Nivea.'

This kind of nasty business shouldn't come up in the techno comic at all.

The techno comic should present arguments about enzymes and electrons, let's say, and you could switch back and forth between them lightning fast and microscopically. Or the dialogue could jump between the bass speakers and the fog machine or between different glasses and drinks and lights.

A coke sachet stuffed scrupulously between credit card and ID would naturally tell a different story from some other bag of cocaine lolling around inside some jacket, not to mention a completely different drug.

The floor tiles would bet against one another about who will get stepped on first by whom, or against one of the thick pillars in the middle of the room about what track will come up next, or the pillars would talk about the guests leaning against them, about their chitchat, and so on and so forth.

That would be one mad freedom of expression.

Then again –

The others showed back up. – The question about the time:

'What time is it?'

'What?'

Wirr tried to say something, his look wandered through the dancers to the other end of the room. An observation dropped in and then scurried off.

And I thought, in individual words: 'Disorientation, – comma, dash – , colon: PLEASANT. Exclamation point!' But just then, at that moment, it was too tedious to note it down. And yet, the entire disorientation-pleasure word sequence as well as the words designating the punctuation marks reappeared several times explicitly in the interior of my head, in my brain somewhere, in correlation with the act of not-noting-down. Until I got it.

'You laughing?'

'Yeah, I – doesn't matter.'

'What?'

An oldie came on. Go. The dance floor filled up. Wirr went too and again as he danced felt at once the pleasant sensation of being moved on all sides: thoroughly shaken and flooded throughout with the substances of movement and music. Again he watched the women, how they lived differently in their bodies, which were them, how they moved them differently, playfully. Maybe with greater pleasure?

The music: something new was happening, the oldie had ended. I looked at the DJ. There was Felix's face, deep in concentration, Alex was standing next to him.

Now new frequencies dropped in, a dense instance of multiple layers rose up, of contradiction and maximum expectation. What will come of it? An immense tumult and affluence of sounds, timed perfectly in their newness, in the transformation into the alterity of the novel sentimental values the upcoming track contained.

Brilliant, really cool.

Dancing girls and faeries shouting.

Dancers shouting.

Every mix was also a small complete self-sufficient self-enclosed artwork.

I saw Max's face, and I was happy.

We were walking in the icy wind one time in January in Chicago, headed towards Lake Michigan, talking about writing and music. We'd got lost, first we were somewhere downtown and then all of the sudden we were high in the sky on the edge of one of those freeway interchanges who knows how many levels up and we couldn't get back down.

The difficulty was a fundamental one: how would a text about our lives have to sound? I had a sort of inkling of sound inside me, a bodily sensation that writing had to articulate.

a kind of: Ave –

'Ave Maria, gratia plena.'

Something along the lines of: bene –
    benedictus –
    you been –
    and the benediction amid your bodies –

And so the fact is you have to wade in, in the literal sense of the term, that's what Albert said to me one time. You couldn't get the text by just starting with the meaning, it had to be conceived differently, through prayer, through the endless iterative pronunciation of the words with the mouth, becoming as it were part of the words oneself by speaking.

'What?'

That was how the thought happened. That was how everyone always made it happen.

DARK

Another fraction of a second made way for another activation pattern, released through some internal or external channel, to rise up, pop, and elapse in a brain.

Aftermath: Hate and hatehate.

'Once the hate-machine is turned on for the first time, you can't turn it back off,' Max said recently to me in a Thomas Bernhard tone, totally hot under the collar.

'Precisely.'

So then: there's all this mad stupid babble, loads of it, above all in the nightlife, of course, about music. About labels, DJs, styles, lines, sounds. As soon as you post up next to someone who for some reason thinks he's intelligent, you're disappointed to hear him blurt out his super-mega-interesting divergent opinion.

You just don't want to hear it. You've heard it a hundred times, read it a thousand, heard it recited already on *House Attack* in the exact same words for ten years, it's been around forever at Rex too, at Focus, every four weeks, there it is like breaking news in *Der Stern*: Electronica, super-serious stuff.

It's boring. Hello! Cut it out!

Mille Plateaux, I know. A Thousand Plateaus, same difference.

Actually, just ONE plateau would be enough, if you could scale it completely, one real proper plateau. If you could at least get to the top of one, starting with your basic mental configuration.

But given that there are people who still have never seen even one single thought from within –

No, I do know them, I do, from the TV, I can't even tell you anymore how many times I've seen these Schepanskis and Ovals and Mouse on Mice and whatever the rest of all these morons are called on TV droning on with their namby-pamby nonsense, a million times, they're all so insanely hollow, a normal person just can't imagine it, actually –

That these people, even more so than before, can palm off their mediocre records on a clientele feverish in their perpetual longing for signs from some sort of intelligent resistance by the mere droning repetition of a word like Deleuze.

That is downright horrible, repulsive, alarming, that is quite simply not to be believed.

Whereas I, on the other hand, actually –

Really?

ME TOO

Yeah?

Wirr made the opposite movement, Laarman didn't react. He was concentrating on Schütte, Schütte on the equipment in the corner. The fuckups were focusing on him. The woman from before had vanished. I would have liked to see that one another time, just briefly: the wisp of fuzz on the upper lip, the dark little hairlets. Or was that only an image-memory-construct based on false enchantment?

I tugged at Sigi, who turned around. Wirr said something, Sigi answered. Wolli put down his glass. Sigi made a defiant gesture. Me: 'I'm coming with.'

Then they set off with daisies in their hands, the so-called flashlight gang.

'All that,' I said to Sigi on the long walk downstairs to the bathroom –

The phrase broke off.

And I said: 'What I wanted to say – '

And then I thought: 'No-one has ever written 'go along' on his highly private flag that he and he alone follows. No, everyone follows his own 'me alone.' And yet all of us are just going along, or aren't we?'

Meantime –

This image was still there, me back in the Ultraschall, it was brand new at the time, standing at the DJ booth and watching Electric Indigo from the wings doing an absolutely sensational set, and suddenly, for the first time, everything hit me and I thought: 'Crazy, this can't real, this is all completely NEW to me, the dissidence-consensus-prohibition is nonsense,' and so forth and so on –

we had gone one and a half steps at most further down through the rumble of the bass.

Sigi turned around to me and laughed.

'Me too.'

The other, over and again, was the beloved older brother, who would pop up now and then from his wondrous world of self-absorption and look at you with friendly eyes, and you were happy and nodded and you said, ardently, just as always, that 'Yeah, right, me too, me too' of yours.

'You shouldn't do that.'

'Why not?'

How do you interpret the findings?

THEORY

Then: brief consultation, buy more beers. The words 'Read the Bible,' read in some book, occurred to me in front of the cigarette machine.

Then a girl gave me a French kiss, passionate, for fun. A riposte to my question of why she smelled so good, so sweet.

She played the give-it-a-go game with me. I was supposed to be the boytoy, she had a piercing on her tongue. She told me her perfume was Lagerfeld and was called *Sun, Moon, and Stars*. Since I had asked her that before.

'I did?'

'Yeah.'

'I don't have the slightest memory of it.'

'Cool.'

'Maybe I was drunk.'

We walked past René and Pete, who were standing in the corner with the Spiegel TV people and gabbing.

34

René and Pete, two young adjunct lecturers from the Berlin Hardwax professorship, always wear their hunting knives in leather sheaths on their belts. That's practical, in case you ever have to unscrew a record. Or for the turntable, if you need to drop it down or speed it up.

'René and Pete,' I told Sigi, 'had to do this bullshit on Spiegel television yesterday, they were blurred out, they masked their voices, and backstage, when the pyro was supposed to go off, the second Spiegel guy was wanting to film through the woman's legs straight across to the other side of the room and zoom in on the two faces, until they were so close that they were like blurred all over again.'

So naturally there was a lot to talk about there.

Their producer said his name was Bernd. That was his company's name, too. Recently they did a series of drug movies about drugs among different social groups: doctors, rockers, homosexual priests. No-one knew the numbers, but they were huge, and Bernd was on it.

Debate in the Bundestag, inquiries in the Council of Elders, conference of the G-7 member states about the drastic plunge of worldwide cocaine prices, and so on.

Stefan Aust: 'We can't do anything about it.'

Jens from Bernd: 'Good, then I'm going straight to Pro Sieben.'

Hans Helmut Kirch: 'Bought and paid for.'

Till from Bernd: 'Right on.'

In Madeira they wrap things up with a handshake, the way men do. Now René and Pete are insistent.

'We're not signing that.'

'Who?'

And twenty years ago at that. A deal's a deal.

We drink, we get closer. Schnapps. We all agree: brotherhood, now. Sven and Till from *Bernd* hug the people from Spiegel TV and René and Pete and everyone hugs them back.

Do big things, go big, make it big, get in, get your big break, and get out. Biolek, Willms-Willemsen, the works.

The next mix flops too. Is anyone paying attention?

In the basement, a whole different party's going on. The way to the bathroom is blocked.

Theory of mixing.

'Come on!'

CANDLES IN UPROAR

The way to the bathroom was blocked. Next mix. They wriggle up toward you, they eye you up in a fluster.

To the chick in the Kookaï top: 'Take it all off, you and me gotta talk!'

In the swamp on the ground in the back, the tribal council is in session.

Below, the men sit and smoke. Above, the young women stand there with their faces.

Hallelujah.

All at once, I can't get the word 'discord' out of my head.

36

The toilet is deep underwater. Crouch in front of the stall. Wait, lurk, rummage in my trousers. One of them pulls me in behind her, shuts the door, starts feeling me up and even kissing me, truth be told. I've known her since the dawn of time. I even took a shower with her naked once, in the staff showers at Gyani's place at the old gunpowder depot, the Pulverturm. She had this teensy adorable little puff of pubic hair on her muff. Her belly, my belly. Her spit in my mouth. I even used to be in love with her, for real, some time back.

Did you see Bernd Eichinger in those denim overalls on Harald Schmidt?

'Discord.'

Wet – not bad – nah, nice – nice

Olaf was taking a piss standing next to Wirr and outlining experiential values in terms of dosage techniques and their pharmacological rationales. Then we walked back upstairs, to the front bar first, to Susi, to drink Averna.

'Susi, three Avernas, please.'

The World as Will and Representation by Franz Schopenhauer.
    'Can a person not bitch?'
    'Nah, nah.'
    'See.'
    'Look.'
    'Right.'
    'Definitely.'

'Maybe that one first.'
'True.'

THE COCAINE OF GOD

Meet girls.
    Take drugs.
    Listen to music.

That was the plan. We even made a wager. Isn't that right, Pascal?

Out of the back room. Tomorrow the rags are getting washed.

ON EARTH

The dealer is there. A bell rings, a lamp flickers, the car door shuts.

    The dealer is there.

    Broken purity, purified and blissful brokenness mingled with the will to euphoria, sobriety, angst. Hard to grasp what the will wants, what it still wants, what it wanted yesterday. On Wednesday there were thoughts and plans about the weekend to come, Wednesday thoughts of a Wednesday brain still banged up a bit from the weekend before.

    What kind of thoughts were those again, exactly? Not a resolution to abstinence, not overtly, anyway, just the indefinite intention to take things a little easier in the near future, in general, as far as the technique of going out and the like. Flimsy thoughts, actually, if you looked at them closely, demented thoughts in retrospect, if we might be more or less blunt. 'What do you say?'

'How many?' 'Five.' 'OK.'

'How much?' 'Come on, now.' 'What do you mean?'

'It's a present from me.'

'A PRESENT?'

Now you could naturally get all squirrely, smell danger of some kind or other, envision yourself lucidly in a lavishly cheap film where Lee's dealer, proverbial smile on his face, gives his former best customer a little something free of charge JUST FOR A MOMENTARY KICK so that from tomorrow on he can maybe become his formerly former best and now once more paying customer again and so on and so on.

Or else you could act like a reasonable grown-up and politely accept what is offered to you and make things easy like everybody else – and that's hard enough. Good.

'Yeah, good, thanks a lot.'

'No problem, be in touch.'

'Will do, ciao.'

'Project: thick skin' I thought succinctly, and walked back to the group from before. Crossing the dance floor, I had that almost forgotten feeling again: 'At this moment, I am apprehending every sentence uttered and or glance anchored in this space.'

This social ailment was a perceptual disorder provoking an aggressive deluge of impressions and reflections and consequently numbly stationary action-congestion-spasms, spazzing out, in other words. I said to Max, 'My reflexes are busted, practically every single one.'

Used to be being busted like that could at least get you a rather remunerative bit of spaz-capital. But alas, thank god, those days are over now. Pathetic.

I saw Wolli talking with René Vaitelje and Tom and Thomas. The one-time champions of the social world had a nasty accident at work this past year. More than one doctor is concerned for his life.

I was thirsty and felt too sober.

I smoked a cigarette, walked to the bar, and heard shouts from all sides.

This guy next to me looked at his phone display glimmering cool green in his hand.

In essence, the truth was this: the cliques were done for, best friendships broken, couples married years before dragged themselves like broken spectres through the night. Deep cavities were bored into the brains of all involved.

Life-cavities in brains all around.

We grabbed onto the bar and kept drinking. The last shred of dignity was: not to give up yet. To keep going like before. To act like it was nothing.

'The state of splinteredness.'

The old clubs were played out and no-one cared anymore about new ones with new concepts from old people. Millennium, Fat Fugo, Studio, Sonic, Atomic. Big time operations, dope clubs, no customers.

The DJs had all played everywhere a hundred times already and everyone had seen and heard or else skipped out on everyone and everything a hundred and one times.

It didn't matter.

It was agony.

40

You could see it, but you couldn't really grasp it.

Everyone everywhere was talking about it: the crucial year. 'The crucial year is coming,' they said everywhere, 'hop or pop, flop or top.'

Later I was standing in the tumult, and my fountain pen scurried blue across the quivering paper in front of me.

I HEARD A LOT ABOUT YOU

The villain stepped aside. The pillar tipped over. The woman from before, with the hillocks, materialized in the new light.

Hillocks.

That's what they called this beautiful landscape where the world welled soft and round and not too huge and an enchanting dew-fresh scent filled the flowers. – A white men's shirt, large, the Indian girl's nose. – She stretched out both arms, the better to wave to me. We talked about white underwear. Now and again, the flat of her hand rested on my covered chest.

We lit each other's cigarettes and drank from our drinks. The vibrating black light strobe was going too.

ADOLF HEALER

Dark tapped the dude behind me on the shoulder, and when he turned, his back jostled us and we jostled the people around us.

Typical greeting, typical hello.

Collective movement to the left, towards the back left corner of the bar. The brokebusted so-called cocaine apparatus was sitting there just then. A moment before they had been scrounging cocaine groupies and at last they had reached cocaine countess maturity-status. There was a time when all we did, especially on Sundays and Mondays, was go to the Einser, which was already played out by then, to have a few beers and laugh at the cocaine countesses and their cocaine countess hysteria.

Pia, Jale, Kessi, and Nicole caught Dark's scent and stalked behind him with a grimace, with a shriek, with a wobble towards the office.

A voice: 'Who?'

Kessi: 'Yeah!'

Pia came back and lit a cigarette. Sigi looked away. She bumped him. 'Warning, Sigi, blab attack.' – An eminently broad and hollow empty nose from the cocaine apparatus, a brutal unbounded unstoppable unhinged text-generating text-machine revving up for whoever came along.

Pia: 'I know you, like, think I'm dumb but – '

'Drop it, Pia, it's cool.'

'But you won't give anyone a chance to – '

Sigi gave Pia a hug.

'A person can change, too.'

'Right, it's OK.'

'No!'

Sigi: 'Just let it go for once, please!'

But then she really picked up steam: she was off the drugs, it had been a few weeks now already, nobody would believe that coming from her, but she didn't need them anymore anyway, it was going to screw up everything for her, with the younger people, right, they couldn't even party anymore without getting wrecked, she'd never seen or been involved with anything like it, a nasty bunch, this crew. All you had to do was look around at all of them –

Then she made a forlorn gesture out over the heads of those around her.

Brief silence.

And she broke out in tears. O God.

Howl, tremble, snivel.

Pia: 'Take a look around, look at how fucked everyone here is!'

You couldn't help but scream, a sensitive type like her just had to howl because it really was that sad, there was something about it that was just so miserable, so fucked, were we not capable of seeing that. 'Or does it not even matter to you or are you just so jaded that you don't even see it anymore or what?!'

And so on and so forth etc.

I said to Sigi: 'There's people that feel pity over something like this.'

He said to Jochen: 'Hey, Jochen, you tosser, come and get us out of here. Thanks!'

'Hey Sascha.'

'Hey Tobi.'

'Hey Tom.'

'Hey Bill.'

Bill: 'We should take these freaky mushrooms now, a little bit at a time.' Word had it they were top notch shit.

'Nice idea, here.'

ALP

Schmalschleger lowered his hairy head down towards us from way up high and opened his mouth and something came out. We looked at each other and had no idea what he was saying. We laughed, he laughed.

The pink plants danced.

Anki said she was going to wander around among the dense ferns. She took me by the hand and led me through the fog. On one side was the entrance to the Wurzelbau, in front of it, blue stones streaked with purplish red veins. The sheen and glimmer of glow-worms hovered nearly immobile in the air, mostly around knee height. You could almost see them shifting in time with the music, or... Maybe not?

I was telling Wolli about this cold damp night way up in the Swiss Alps when everyone had dropped acid.

The acid freaks had gaudy leggings pulled up over their spindly withered little legs, paper lanterns bobbed over the dance floor, the idiots and acrobats onstage were thrashing around in splendid clothes on ropes and poles, and the acid freaks looked at you like frantic driven festive furies, bemused glances crumbling from their fluttering eyes. Bizarre scene.

Acid is kind of like a strange religion. Hard stuff. Really, from the ranks of the drug burnouts, those were the most burnt out of all, the acid burnouts, the enlightened ones.

But even more absurd and busted than that already despicable drug burnout was, obviously, all-embracing abstinence. The in principle programmatic resolution in favour of sobriety, the decision, as a matter of principle, NOT and never ever to take something bad, that was outright cretinism. Not to take drugs, and not to do so as a matter of principle, is absolutely, without room for doubt, the bustedest thing of all.

44

There are actually people who as a matter of principle don't even drink: no alcohol, just cola, cherry juice, Bitter Lemon.

Weed: out of the question.

Meat: the decline of the west.

Cocaine: never before five.

Heroin: only on the weekend, to loosen up after the cocaine.

Aspirin: better not, supposedly it's bad for your stomach.

Antibiotics: don't you have something natural instead?

Prozac: honestly, we'd try all the legal stuff if only it actually did something. But is there really any point?

So what about a majestically murky near-death experience on ketamine? I'll go ahead and prep the needle.

Fucked up scene, no?

Fucked up, totally fucked up.

'What can I get you?'

'A water, please.'

'Water, of course. Sparkling or still?'

'Sparkling makes me burp.'

'Oh, well!'

'For real.'

'Oh yeah.'

'Right.'

'Yeah!'

'And so?'

'Water, still water, please.'

Here we have the people who feel called to write features for their daily feature editor: about the night and the nightlife, fashion and music. Or raw direct teeming vivacious breakneck storyteller literature, like my friend

Maxim 'You have to slag off your friends with all your strength, constantly, otherwise you feel all old and sad' Biller. Used to be a normal guy, now he's a teetotaling non-smoker and a super serious solemn raconteur honing his short and long stories.

'People, awaken!' I said to Moritz at his cocktail hour at the Greek standing bar at the Südfriedhof to celebrate his departure from the *SZ*. And I tried, just a wee bit drunk, to say the same to the *BR-Youth*-TV-moderator, Uli or Susi or Sigi or whatever her name was.

Obviously obliviously she'd blurted out the word 'pussy' in the very first phrase she addressed to me, and exposed me to it with her pronunciation, with her mouth. Naturally that struck her as weird now, as she turned around in front of me, snugly packed in her tight jeans and rather cute with a new haircut, super sober, nice and nimble. – I was into it.

While the others were dancing their acid-truth-dance on the alp, outdoors amid the icy stone, where a night-white-glaring, full-moon-spotlight shone, we crept, shit-faced and shivering, into the big tent at some late hour and got under other people's blankets and sleeping bags, squeezed together tight, and fell into the deep, grunting, and stertorious sleep of the sodden.

When we woke, it was another day –
On the other hand –
But then again –

Strangely though, you can't say anything good about drugs, either, if you do, the effect is right away perverse, cultish. As though you were praising the wonders of oxygen in the air or the bewitching beauty of the nude bodies of eleven-, twelve-, thirteen-year-old girls or boys.

You hear it and you think: this one's off his rocker.

THE BRICKLAYER'S BOOK

Now the girls wanted to scram. – Where to? Why? What for? – In the interim, the music had apparently turned lame, or way too hardcore, or just dull, or something.

'This music's irritating,' Kessi said to Pia.

Pia: 'This atmosphere is shit.'

Jale: 'There's the after-hours antisocial types.'

Mike asked: 'Already?'

And Nilly, who had spent the entire evening sitting by the register, nodded dimly.

Mike: 'Where'd they come from?'

'Upstairs.'

'Who was playing?'

'No idea.'

I was dizzyish, but not enough, not really. We sat on the floor, leaned on the wall, watched from below, amused and pleasantly impassive, the woman-frenzy outburst among the women above. Olaf was cradling little Susie in one arm, Jasmin was sitting next to Natalie on his other side, I was next to her, everything super.

Sassy was sitting next to me. Then she stood up, twitched a bit, naturally with ironic intentions, and she looked around with a gently inquisitive look and said: 'Who's rolling?'

Who's rolling?

Who's cutting?

Who's breaking bread?

The hand growing from the end of Olaf's arm

stretched upwards, opened gracefully, took the stuff from Sassy's hand, retracted, and looked around and asked oblivious into the void: 'Anyone got papers?'

Then for a long time nothing else happened.

One corner away, a little group of youngdistraught novicettes and novices were sitting there all knotted together, hands still hot and damp from ecstasy and hearts slightly melancholic, and now the effects of the big drug night are abating slowly; exhausted, obviously, fired up by what they've experienced, coming down now yet still somehow solaced by the bright approach of the new-born morning.

Beautiful sight. For us, anyway, just as beautiful for us, the wrecks and fuckups sitting around with countless fuckups the years had well and truly wrecked. Prudently, the fuckups took a nip of this, helped themselves to a little bit of that.

Quite reasonably.

That was the more or less tragic situation.

'It's not really all that tragic,' I said to Sigi, kissed Natalie on her imperious nose, stood up, and fished out my cigarettes. Pia made the international cigarette moocher's gesture, demanding without uttering a word, and I held my pack out to her. She took one, no *thank you*, goes without saying, and made a nasty remark about the brand, HBs. Cocaine groupie Kessie laughed hysterically.

Lovely company.

Instead of meekly lighting Pia's cigarette as she was pantomiming for me to do, I plucked it from her mouth, swiping my hand an inch away from her face, and lit it for myself.

Then Olaf said: 'Give me a filter.'

I tore off the little fold of cardboard on the flip-top box that the cigarette industry has prepared for just such occasions, rolled it into a tiny tube, and laid it on Olaf's knee.

Then I stood up and laughed. 'It'd be great to go back over to where the music is.'

Walking back, I thought about Angela and the totally fucked up story with the Bricklayer's Book.

THE JOURNEY OF THE GOD OF BLISS

The stream through the hallway carried Wirr off in its calm, unhurried, inwardly surging shoving and strolling, surging and traipsing, tripping and trudging and tumbling and lolling and babbling.

Hall of all halls, gates to eternity.

New, anew, newly new once more, new, unseen and unforeseen: people coming towards you.

You, my dear kindly ones, madness, pff.

Some sort of effect seemed once more to rise to the surface from the depths of years and hours past. The colours of the clothing and fabrics shone here in the light more extreme than at night, the bodies showed through the clothes.

Wirr saw faces facing him, gazes adjudging his gazes, reflecting him, somehow. But what he grasped, quick and fleeting and evernew, eluded any quick categorization. And why?

I stayed standing there briefly, looked at the floor, reached my hands up high over my head towards the sky and shouted:

'Sup?!'

Then I looked back up, took a hard deep breath, and accepted the mercifully friendly responses from my immediate surroundings as an homage to a monarch who alas was going gaga or maybe already had been dotty since way back when.

'There you have it,' I murmured, and walked off.

'You know *Walking* by Thomas Bernhard?'

Or *Playing Watten?*

Rotten spruce, gravel pit, and barracks.

Dear Sir. – Decrepitude I, Decrepitude II, Decrepitude III.

Then we give everything a quick once-over, Wolli and I. We end up all by ourselves deep down in the guts of the establishment at a beer table in a bare-bones stark empty room next to one of the offices. Wolli was talking about the arrest the day before yesterday.

'So they locked up Stefan's stuff in the evidence room. And I was like: OK, got it. So they've finally cleaned him out. Then comes a brief back and forth about Jens's black bag. About if they'd gone through it already or not. They'd already gone through it, nothing to see there. They let him take it with him.

Then they sat us back down. And we had to deal with each other. Like: "Don't move!" ha ha.

It was obvious at that point we were driving to their station. And I asked the guy: "Right, how long is that going to take then?"

"Yeah, not so long. Two hours at most."

And I thought to myself, what kind of sense of time does this guy have. It was already past five-thirty.

OK then. So then the question was: who's driving who? And when? And how and all that. And then two of us took off, me first, I think. Or was Jens the first one? Nah, I think I was the first to head out.'

'Did you go in the paddy wagon or in the unmarked car?'

'Nah, it was chill, this totally chill Golf GTI. "The back door jams a little. Hit the guardrail going 160. Had to ride it out." – He told me in Bavarian thieves' cant.

So then I just got in the back and on the way to the – we're talking behind the Circus Krone – '

'You buy yourself some Stuyvesants?'

'Nah. They had – this was at the Thai takeout joint where we went with Martin – so I said: "Lucky Strikes." He thought I said Winstons and he brought me Stuyvesants. That was honestly stellar. He says: "Winston? Winston." And I'm like: "Yeah, yeah, OK." He brings Stuyvesants. That was the shit.'

'So then you went to the station?'

'Then we went to the station. The whole way the dude's trying to wheedle something out of me, like where's techno come from, K and all that. He's like itching to know. And I'm like: "Yeah, uh, um..." OK: but this dude says: "You talking acid, or...?" "Yeah, yeah, exactly." I couldn't believe it. Then he asked where the DJs all come from. And I broke it down to him briefly how people just kind of know and all that. Laid it out for him. Probably he knew all that anyway.

So the thing is, like he was pretty cool, the dude.'

'What'd he look like?'

'Ponytail in the back, bald on top, *skullet*, you know

that one, he kept it covered up with a stocking cap though. I didn't see it till later. Thirty, early thirties.'

'I know that dude.'

'Yeah? You know him?'

'I think so.'

'Name's Jäger. That was the guy who handled me, Jäger's his name. Ha ha ha, for real.'

'There's not really many people who just rock a bald spot like that, with a tonsure and all. And a bummy rat tail like that in the back.'

'Honestly he was kind of cool.

Ah, right! They'd already gone through the car before we took off. THAT was a stunt. That was why it took so long. By then Jens was already elsewhere.

So: they had to search the car. Yeah, I was supposed to come along. "So, hm? should he come, too?" "Yeah, maybe." "That way you won't go saying afterwards we planted something on you." Honestly though, I think that was one of their jokes.

So now we're back downstairs. We go over to the ratty green Benz. They were like: "It's a little grubby." Then they poked all through it.

Finally they opened the glass crate from the glass market. They looked all through it. They found the pills, the vitamin C tablets. You can read it right there, Ascorbic Acid, or something like that. Or maybe it doesn't even say Ascorbic. The point is, it has Acid on it. He couldn't grasp that. He had it there in front of him the whole time, he was rubbing it between his fingernails, smelling it and all. It was fine, honestly.

In the trunk I've got the champagne and the schnapps

and all the posters. That was crazy too. He can't take his eyes off the glue. Like so. Keeps like trying to get a whiff of it. So I was like: "Glue, for the posters." Then he keeps moving the paste back and forth right in front of him. He's staring at it like he's panning for gold or something. At last we all agreed it really was poster glue. And not like, uh, a bowl of ecstasy. Or whatever. In the bucket for picking mushrooms.

Honestly my ride was DIRTY as all get out. And the boys kept on digging through all the shit but were less and less motivated.

And then they pull out another bag. One of those jute shopping bags for hippies, those anti-plastic things, FREAKING nasty, it had all these old plastic bags inside that Inge must have packed in there. And the dude actually reaches in with his fingertips, all grossed out. So I was like: "I think that's just trash."

I wanted to get rid of the thing. But there was nothing to do about it. They start acting all weird because I want to toss it. So I was like: "Fine, whatever, I'll throw the thing away later." And I threw it into my car and shut the door. Real firm.

I still had 600 marks in the car, rolled up. "I suppose that's change for your club?" the guy says. I'm there with these dudes by the car and Jens is long gone.

Wait, is that right?

But I was still sitting down in the corridor when he came through.

Right, right, so he was still there then, yeah. Because we were still trying to arrange where to catch up with each other later. And there was no way, because we just couldn't think of anywhere. So we finally said OK, we'll hit up Babalu and we'll work something out there.

Right, so then we headed to the feds' office. There they got these cool cards that they hold out like this. And they start reading.

Then the door opens up.'

We drink another coffee in the side room. Then we go back upstairs. Anja, Anne, and Nadja are standing there. They're hawking the new *Raveline*: 'Big Westbam article, *Raveline* here, free!'

The chicks are loaners from the Hamburg women's-irony-rag *Envy* and they have no doubt they are off the chain. They think of themselves as artists and girlfriends and they're wearing these skimpy red and white and black threads, 'Leather and Latex!' they keep screeching that out, too. 'Inside Fetish Story!' they shout, 'Get your sex report right here!' Then they squeeze their breasts together with both hands until the cleavage is just this teensy-weensy crack and they push them out like Diane Brill for all the world to see and the ravers just shuffle past unimpressed.

For tubby little Anne, the desired effect wasn't long in coming. Anne's idea is to use her so-called 'tits' in a targeted manner to make it to boss at *Vogue* one day. She's already writing fashion articles for *Praline*, *Gala*, *Spex*, and *Die Akutelle*, under a pseudonym, of course. Isabelle has commissioned a more theoretically oriented report from the three of them for *Texte zur Kunst* about Mayday fashion. Isabelle is crazy about fashion. 'Ulf is into it, too' Anne adds.

Anja and Nadja jump on the display table, spread their legs, shout 'Pussy Power Galore!' and make the proper corresponding movements. Sex, fun: you get the point, women emboldening one another. A beautiful thing, and for a good purpose.

The music drops out, the scene dies down, the women clatter off the table. A dude with a 'tache makes his way to the mixer, the editor-in-chief of *Raveline*. What's his name again? The women sip bubbly out of plastic cups.

Geri shows up. She's here for the agency. She gets a glass of bubbles too and in exchange has to hear from the others about the invitation to *Liebe Sünde*. The moderator had just come past.

'What's her name again, the thick cockeyed chick that's always got that goofy uptight idle laugh?'

'Verona Feldbusch?'

'No, the other one, the one from the show about the instincts. The one with the sex words. The one who quit.'

'Ah, her.'

'They pay pretty good, too.'

To be continued in DECONSPIRATION.

Wirr looked up, trying to orient himself to his location by the letters. E, F, E, aha. I thought I had to get to G and H. Maybe even to K, all right.

Then Armin and Tilmann came over, looking strange.

Wirr: 'What's up with you two?'

'You didn't hear?'

'No, what?'

'Schütte's done for?'

'What? Done for? What does that mean, done for?'

Schütte had lost it and was down in the cellar somewhere, *Frontpage* was over. Laarmann had gone into hiding, maybe he was on the lam. The Amsterdam Bureau had burned down, a New York lawyer was tying up the last threads, the paperwork, over in Los Angeles. Anyway Tilmann was supposed to snap a big photo spread of the entire disaster for Leber at the *Stern*.

'For real?' Wirr said.

'For real!' Armin and Tilmann echoed in chorus.

'Bullshit,' Wirr said, 'I was just drinking shots with Laarmann and someone from his sweet little Laarmann retinue somewhere in the back.'

'The question is, what does that matter now? All this happened just in the last few minutes, seconds even, maybe.'

'You're nuts, you've lost your minds. Tilmann! Armin!'

'Cool, man, you do your thing!'

'What? What thing?'

'Keep your eyes peeled you don't get caught up in it, Rainald.'

Eyes peeled? So I don't what?

THE GALL.

Food smells, pizza, sausage, mustard, roast.

Question: Hungry?

Nah, not really.

'Any chance you've seen Robert around anywhere?'

'Robert? Which Robert? Our Robert, Robert from Munich?'

'No, the one from Mannheim.'

'I don't even know him.'

'Ah, OK, it's just we lost him right around here somewhere.'

'Got it.'

'No big deal. Thanks anyway. I just thought you knew him too.'

'I don't think so.'

'OK, well, if you see him, he's got on like a T-shirt, I mean like a shirt with – '

'I don't think I know you guys either.'

'Oh. Sorry, we must have got mixed up then.'

'No probs.'

'Where you from?'

'Munich.'

'Munich! I was there one time!'

'Cool.'

'Yeah, at Rave City last year. Where you headed now?'

'I was thinking of going to the other hall.'

'Dude, nice, I'll come with if that's cool. The rest of you coming?'

'Where?'

'Over to the other hall.'

'Why not? Isn't Woody up next there?'

'Right!'

'Cool!'

There was a bottleneck a few feet further on. Deadlock and rubbish. Probably the hallway that led over to the *Viva* stand.

At *Viva* the critical techno presenter Sascha Kösch and his girlfriend and co-presenter Mercedes Bunz were standing by the Cola machine. This was dirty commercial chicanery, they thought, having cola here, COLA in capital letters front and centre, like Cola was buying off the presenters and giving them away, to weaken and secretly corrupt them, most likely.

'I'm denouncing this,' said Sascha Kösch.

'We have absolutely got to bring this up later in the broadcast,' said Mercedes Bunz.

He looked at her tenderly, she looked at him more

tenderly. They looked at each other so tenderly it hurt. That works, you just have to want it. Theirs was cool egalitarian relationship, they thought and did loads together.

Sascha Kösch: 'Best thing would be to also do a big story about it for *Spex*. I'm gonna call Gurke first thing tomorrow morning.'

Then they walked over to the makeup tables. They were totally against this commercial, capitalist makeup routine.

Mercedes Bunz to the makeup artist: 'Make us up to look critical, please, so the brainlessness isn't so obvious.'

The makeup artist: 'I would have thought there was still a little bit of brain in there.'

Sascha Kösch: 'Likeliest thing is this vile cola industry assault has already torn it out by the roots.'

End of the comic.

On the title page, the title: *The Self-Righteousness Radicals Ride Again. And This Time, We Shoot Back.* – There's gotta be time for that.

The coloured lights fired up, the *Viva* fans screeched behind the balustrade: 'Viva *Viva*!' and the interview got underway. Sabine Christ asked Kid Paul, Paul M. here, about his new underground Berlin label, Ism Productions.

'Hello, Paul!'

'Hello, Sabine!'

'How's it going?'

'Good, how about you?'

'Good as well, thanks.'

'Nice to hear.'

'Yes. So we ought to get started.'

'Great idea.'

'You've stopped playing, you've dropped your old name, stopped going out at night, for some time now you've even stopped buying the latest records. Might we say you've grown up?'

'Looks almost just like in real life, right?' said Jana. And Desiree said: 'I think I hear your pager going off again.'

They moved away from the group of female onlookers the hand camera had just filmed, and Desiree rooted around inside the plush teddy bear Jana was sporting as a backpack on her back for the beeper; in the interim it had started beeping rather loudly.

'What's it say?'

Desiree handed the little pink gadget to Jana, who looked at it and got spooked.

All at once there was a guy standing right there next to them, just too big in general, his face too fleshy, the guy must have been some kind of goon.

Jana: 'What's this idiot want?'

Him: 'My name's Alfred Steffken, and apparently you're the ones I've been looking for.'

'For us?'

'Apparently?'

'Aren't you Desiree and Dana?'

'Nope.'

The guy stopped, wavered a moment, and the girls beat it out of there. Jogging along, Jana: 'That was that dumbfuck photographer.'

'No way, that dude's name's Steffen.'

'That's what he said.'

'That's not what he said.'

'Anyway, he looked like a plainclothes copper.'

'I'm not one though,' said this so-called Alfred

Steffken, jogging up awkwardly behind the girls. 'I'm a photographer. People say I'm the worst photographer in Germany.'

'Super. If it works for you.'

'So what do you want with us?'

'I'm friends with Herbert Breitenhauer, the guy that just beeped you. He gave me the number 220. I'm supposed to say it to you all.'

Actually Jana had got a 412 message about this 220-friend with the code 108 from Herbert, that was code for 'it's OK', her display showed the numbers: '412:220:108.'

'Cool, that's right. So what can we do for you?' Jana said, acting tartish.

Desiree: 'Nude photos? Portrait photos, maybe? Fashion photos? Art photos? Porno, sex, erotica, white trash, art-art, name your poison, Mr Steffken.'

'To tell the truth, I wanted to buy some cocaine. Three grams, if possible.'

'Three grams? You serious?'

'Could be two.'

'Cocaine, aha.'

'What might three grams cost?'

They were roaming through an empty room with corny music blaring. At the DJ stand: a cute little poodle, now that is amusing. Maybe one from the Golden Poodle Club in Hamburg? In the corner: women, budding *Butz*-editors and other so-called 'journalists' flashing their little plastic passes, which read: 'No idea whatsoever about anything at all.' You can't get in without this pass. They check them at the door. Also important: you need to be ready to pronounce the words 'Drum and Bass' with absolute clarity.

Cut up pointlessly, one after another, pointless records are spinning. The poodle hasn't got a clue how to mix. Doesn't matter though, babe, he doesn't have any idea about anything anyway. Same as everyone else, his relationship to music is primarily anecdotal, he's heard this about that, picked this up from so-and-so. Even spinning he approaches from a more activist angle. Headphones on and off, twist the knobs a bit. Almost actually looks legit, right?

He concentrates on trying to look concentrated on something here and there. Concentrate? If only I knew on what, the poodle tells himself.

The poodle is pleased with himself.

Poodle art: girly art.

Jasmin is finally done with work. She's sitting with her friend Johanne on the cable drums in the back. Johanne looks like proper shit, a timid ugly duckling. Opens her mouth, pesters. Jasmin: cute, quick, lucid. Successful. A winner. Johanne idolizes Jasmin like mad. Together the two of them make a cool couple of besties.

Jasmin started working with *Viva* recently, on the call-in show at nine at night. Her big role model is Heike, of course. Heike's got a cool career behind her, she thinks, and wishes her all the best for the future.

Jasmin is now telling Johanne the latest news. Of course that means: whatever has happened in the last seven or so minutes of both of their so-called 'love lives'. This demands ten minutes' worth of discussion. Jasmin leads an insanely thrilling life.

At first she just had two little things going on right then, one in France and another one from way way back at home not far from Leipzig. Then she met this dude

Ken in the early morning hours at the Comet Awards where she was cutting interviews for *Viva* with Tommy and Sabine, right away all shameless and super-cute this Ken up and pulls her away.

She's all insecure and inhibited since she started doing TV, she doesn't know anymore whether the people are interested in her TV face or in the person she really is. With Ken it's different. He doesn't have cable and doesn't even know she does TV.

They hang out the rest of the night.

Afterwards weeks passed, and she had almost forgotten the thing with Ken when she ran into him again in Munich at P1, where she was recording a pilot for a new club show for *Viva*. Ken is obviously pissy about the wrong number she gave him, so she lies, says it was a mix-up or misunderstanding. And that night they have a blast together again.

Next morning she's got to fly back to Cologne real early, and before noon she's called Johanne, who's supposed to get Ken's number.

Ken's still sleeping, he hears it ringing, lets the answering machine pick up, and half-groggy he hears Jasmin leave him a halfway-earnest declaration of love on the answering machine, and she tells him her number and says he HAS TO call her. 'Cause of love. Then she flies to Marseille to see Sabeth, the boyfriend she's got there.

Early in the morning on the plane to Cologne she's decided to break things off with Sabeth, because honestly, it doesn't make sense anymore, because really, she isn't in love with him anymore. And then that night they're sitting in a cosy restaurant in the harbour and all of a sudden it feels like a totally pointless scandal to bring this closeness to an end.

Plus the lust. They sleep together.

And just afterwards, side by side with Sabeth, she is totally sure for real now though that she is totally in love with Ken.

Next morning she's got to record the show, so she drives straight from the airport to the studio.

She doesn't get home till late at night.

She's got eight messages on the machine, two anonymous, three from Wilgins, Sabrina begging several times for her to call her back, her manager Claudia, she already handled that, and then of course the by now ritualized declaration of love from Sabeth, which she can't even bear to listen to, she's so bummed out.

So she calls Sabeth and tells him how crazy in love with him she is.

'So what should I do now?' Jasmin asks. And Johanne, who already knows the saga, just repeats back everything Jasmin has just told her, particularly the appraisals and assessments. Jasmin listens to Johanne, nods, and feels one hundred per cent understood. These conversations are super-important for Jasmin. And especially for Johanne.

Fifteen minutes later: Steffken is standing downstairs waiting on the girls on the steps behind the VIP lounge as arranged. The girls make him wait. Steffken gave them 150 marks. If they don't come back, the money's gone. If the cocaine they're selling him isn't cocaine, he won't be so dull tomorrow. If it does come through, well, who the fuck cares.

He picks up a copy of *Groove* that's lying on the floor, sits on the lowermost step, and leafs through it. None of it speaks to him at all. For now, he has nothing in his mind. He flips the pages, waits. Unexpected, unlooked-for, self-awareness breaks in: 'Basically I'm just a good-for-nothing twat.'

Oops. Pardon me? And yet not a single objection rises up anywhere inside Steffken. 'That's just how it is,' he thinks, and right away is punished by Andreas Dorau's fretful voice fretting agonizingly over and over: 'That's just how it is, that's just how it is.'

'Exhausting,' Jana says.

Desiree: 'Weird dude. To be honest, I like *Bamby* better, like a thousand times better.'

Steffken: 'Did it work out?'

They give him a pack, and Alfred Steffken kisses Jana on the cheek goodbye.

Desiree: 'Hey! Security, that weirdo there just gave my friend a dirty kiss!'

The worst photographer in Germany tries to laugh and splits.

Jana: 'I'm excited to hear what Breitenschlager says when he hears the story.'

'Doesn't matter.'

'Look, here comes Dieter Gorny.'

Dieter Gorny drags himself and all his tons of influence with formidable elegance down the stairs. Over his shoulders bob the preposterous tips of the hairs of his so-called Peter Handke haircut.

The ravers are sitting on the steps the way kids back home at school sit on the schoolhouse steps and their motto is: No-one gets through. This world belongs to us. Dieter Gorny digs that. He likes being here being almost one with his cagey clientele.

'There's something sweet and simple and just right about this,' Gorny says to Min Kai, his companion, 'something touching, somehow.'

Min Kai has put on twenty kilos since she's been friends with this Sat-1 gofer.

What's his name again? is the media junkies' mantra.

It's coming to me right now, is the reflex mantra's rejoinder.

Gorny: 'The wooing and tempting begins.'

Min Kai: 'Can you even actually find true love here.'

'I thought you wanted the job no matter what.'

'I thought *Die Welt* was the capital of love.'

Gorny sees himself less as head of a music station than as a grand philosophizing communicator and president of pop ideas. He invented techno all by his lonesome and made it successful and that's why just yesterday the German Academy of Phono and Literature gave him the Golden Gorny Lifetime Achievement Award. The ceremony is taking place a little further back, and again they will announce: 'And the winner is – '

Here a dinner jacket is mandatory.

'Unfortunately I can't let you in like that.'

Peek in real quick over at P1 where Blub Club is supposed to be, or...? Yeah, for sure.

Everyone gets a welcome shot at the entrance and Norbert blesses everyone in a red cardinal's robe with white gloves and a red-and-white mitre sitting big on his head. We walk straight in, and right away you get practically swallowed by this whole immensely elaborate conception of décor: colourful, glowing, dignified: a darkly opulent, queer-Bavarian pop high ministry of the high baroque, medieval songs and monks in cowls, boyish altar boys swinging smoking censers, pews and confessionals, and up front a gold glimmering monstrance and in its glowing white centre the obligatory erect member is unveiled and released for blissful worship.

Very lovely. And the bells toll loud and ominous all round. And the place is packed to bursting and rages in this old, insane way, frenzied around the holy of holies, the sanctum and sacrum, the sex of music.

Old promoter's wisdom: the best décor is a full house. So that means today's décor is optimal twice over. Ali's got the music covered, fully in line with the house style: sex-house-trash-pop, dull, busted, poppy, just as it should be. And in front of him on the dance floor the dancers pump and nudge, shriek and twitter, strut and stamp shoved tight together, and now and then the lights flicker on bright-garish and motley and illuminate the heads and make the faces beam.

I simply cannot get tired of this.

You walk into a place like this, and the effect hits you then and there: Euphoria.

As if you had NEVER felt this before.

As if there were no such thing as the history of happiness.

And since I'm going to the back, to the jam-packed back bar where Wolli and Pedro are serving, I run straight into Ali.

'You spinning today or what?'

'Better believe it!' he says, plants a sweat-damp kiss on my cheek in greeting, hands me one of the two beers he just got from the bar, and hurries off, red-hot, soaking wet, and crows out, without provocation, his insane Ali-laughter.

'Thanks, Ali!'

At the bar: everyone. More or less everyone. Olaf, Anki, Martina, Helli, Sassy, Tommy, Susi, Daniela, Nilly, Virginia, Caro, Kathi, Sascha, Wirna, Silvie, Änni, Dominik, Claudi, Daniel, Sue. Beer please. Thanks. Hey Bob, Kathrin, Cambis, Keiwan, Robert, Pata, Kerstin, Daniel, Thomas, Susi from the crew and little Susi and Fabienne and Natalie and Alex and Felix. I'm gonna dance. Hiya Moritz! Rebecca! Back to the bar: more beer, please. Hey Alex, Sarah, Jerome, Alia, Jenny, Katja, Steffen, Michel, Hartwig. Hey David, Dorle, Upstart, Monika, Lester, Barbara, Aroma, and what do you know, Roy's standing right there. 'Hey, Roy!' – 'Hey, Rainald!' – 'Hey, Hille! You're here, too?!' – 'Yeah, why not? Once in a while, you know. Bea and Cle are here too, upstairs.' For real? Cool.

You wave and laugh with several people, several you just say hello to, many you chat with for a bit. Cool. The hyperpublic locus of night and its cascade of private histories.

Only after the first three, four beers does a mass of life like this start shifting back and forth between the individuals in this way that may be only possible here, in this concentrated and complicitly coded form. Being constantly torn apart, broken, negated by something and stylized in a quite peculiar way.

Subject: life.

People.

Everyone.

And your torment and mine.

'Even the most private accounts of catastrophe,' I

think later, leaning in the corner alone to take a rest and down my umpteenth beer, 'experience a transformation here, via noise and euphoria, into a generic fucked up-ness excluded on all sides from the fucked up-ness that was here the object of jubilation.'

Everyone here acts like everything is different from what it is. That is the enigmatic appeal to the dignity of nocturnal ferment and endless celebration. Its irreducibly local and at the same time, yeah, that's right, *utopian* dimension.

'You, no,' said the bouncer to Tobias Thomas.

Him: 'Why?'

'Just 'cause.'

'You don't even know me.'

'Do too.'

'From where?'

'From right in front of me.'

'So?'

'That's all I need.'

'Come on!'

'That's enough.'

'Redneck!'

'Yeah, yeah,' said Rolli, slammed the door in Tobias Thomas's face, turned around, and lit a cigarette.

The coatroom girl: 'What's with you today?'

'Bunch of retards.'

Rolli's door was the stuff of legend: money, sex, youth. – Scenesters, demimonde, musicians. – DJs, groupies, artists. – Dope fiends and *soi-disant* life artists and unmitigated fuckups. – And from their ranks, only the best, the most beautiful, the most ordinary and the most trenchant. Wherever Rolli was working the door, there was celebration inside, ruthless, at the bar and everywhere till it stopped.

Rolli was naturally a philosopher by trade. Ethnographer of the night, with an inclination towards general and fundamental rules and a will to systematization. He reserved special attention for the college educated of the world: curt and cruel as the situation allowed, he would throw the sober, the amiably hunched over, those whose diffidence manifested a pure, silent megalomania, and of course the super-helpless ones crying for help out on their ear, get outta my sight, scram. Job description: Intellectual debaser. Today again, a glorious bashing of editors, ad men, photographers, and students.

Those who thought they were clever and sensitive were, plain and simple, a little too plain and too simple, too dull, too dumb for Rolli. They couldn't party, they didn't even know what that meant: excess. Boozing, sex, violence. Rolli: no danger, no party; no fear, no fun; no beat, no logic, no nothing. Rolli: Stay at home, you! Sucker! The drug dog barks, the raid is on.

Rolli opened the door and greeted Timo, Hassan, and Arco with a handshake. Polite grunts all round, claps on the back. Please, thanks. How nice: our gang of yugos has finally come through.

A LITTLE NOCICEPTIN?

Jörg Haiser lets Tobias Thomas tell him the story about the door. Jörg Haiser comes up with a little story for the week, this time, unusually, rather critical in its approach. Christoph Gurk from *SZ Magazin* joined in, Lorenz Schröter, *Spiegel Spezial*, Hamburg. Already there: Kristian Gracht, *Die Bunte*, Munich; Patrick Wilder, *Liebe Hiebe*, Berlin.

Distinguished company, spirited debate.

They've known each other for years, respect and detest each other slightly despite having never studied the so-called pieces of their counterparts under the magnifying glass, or even read them for that matter. Don't you already know what's coming when Schröder writes or Heiser talks, when Poschardt starts running off at the mouth again or Pesch fires off another of his studies? Especially as they are exceedingly familiar with the so-called *outlets* the others write for, and in all honesty for ages now the mere act of paging through them, let alone reading them, has been downright unbearable. The papers corresponding to the others have suffered a correspondingly pathetic decline in recent years in comparison to what they were before, to the corresponding outlet one writes for oneself, and so on and so forth.

To be honest, there was a general lack of interest in all the things one had not just written oneself, and it had grown through the years, but with this had come a greater decorum, a rational, slightly cowed mellowness, an initial side effect of continual babble-poison intoxication – an inevitable consequence of sitting there at editing room tables contaminated with babble-poison, withdrawal from the real world, endless paging through every last page, flow and overflow of the printed word and the overflowing of these flows.

The phone was always ringing somewhere: Mr Bidowitsch, lately of *Männer Vogue*, Munich, was there, I don't know if you remember me? You had to constantly phone in, ring up, call back, chitchat right and left. Something always had to be rushed in or out, photos, galleys, breaks, lists, and don't forget the boilerplate.

– Wait a sec, I'll bang out a bit of boilerplate. – I'm calling you about the photos we talked about, is that taken care of?

Wirr: Eh, no, thanks.

'What was that incredibly pertinent thing you said just now?' Mark Terkessides, *Der Prinz*, Hamburg, said to Kristian Gracht, and bowed to him. Gracht was looking pallid today. The eternal confusion was wearing on him: You're the famous Kracht? – No, he's at the *Spiegel*. – Christian Kracht had wrung a super-sweet author contract out of the *Spiegel* that got him right to room and board at that legend of style, the legendary *Spiegel* cafeteria. This clause was a nice touch, above all for retelling. I'm at the *Spiegel* now, but just because of the cafeteria. Soon I'm headed off to Delhi.

Incidentally, Mark Terkessides was working on a book about the history of *Tempo* that would one day bear the stellar title *The Tempo Years*. Those were wild days back then, the eighties, young people today wouldn't know a thing about that, all these people went straight from the school desk to these 5,000-mark-a-month jobs, more actually, if you want to get into specifics, and they hung out and hung around and took drugs and freaked out the old bosses, who were already in their thirties by then. Great. *The Tempo Years* was going to reconstruct all that in detail, like a collective biography of an entire generation, an entire writer-generation that is, if you will.

Terkessides: 'Maybe Moritz von Uslar will join in, too, but then, maybe it's too stupid for him.'

Gracht: 'That's cool and all, but what about Kraftwerk?'

Everyone: 'Dude!' 'Yeah!' 'Kraftwerk!'

Kraftwerk had just played at the Tribal Gathering on the other side. And however much it had actually been shit, the ones who were there to report on it naturally knew beforehand: it had been 'legendary,' of course it had.

Heiser: 'Mythical.'

'Sublime.'

'Incredible.'

'Totally legendary.'

'The second coming, no lie.'

'A divine hour.'

'An epiphany' – etc. etc.

Ulf Poschardt butted in and said: 'The important thing is first of all to accumulate lots of enthusiasm-capital as quickly as possible right there in front of the others, loud as possible. You can draw on that later to puff up your own blowhard text.'

Yes, yes siree. And why not?

Minutes later, hours before.

A little *taz*-thing says suddenly: 'Hours in, drugs taken. Isn't everything easier when duty yields to meaningfulness?'

Right. The third of a third of a pyramid pill split in thirds under the magnifying glass and popped at the wooden table in the little bar next to the big hall. Maybe it was just a poppy seed or a grain of pepper?

Nope.

The lights turned warmer, the bar cosy, everything just a teeny bit softer somehow, warmer, more natural. More normal, actually, you could almost say. What do you mean?

Light-Michi laughed, Pauli, the hairy gypsy, laughed, I laughed, too. Arm and arm we floated in, away into the great main arena.

Lorenz Schröter was standing there directly in front

of us. 'Might you all have taken some drugs?'

'Drugs?'

'Yeah, you all look like you – '

Us: 'We thought it was forbidden to take drugs.'

Him: 'Yeah, right, but – '

Us: 'Excuse me, but you wouldn't by any chance be employed as a police officer by the police department?'

Him: 'Nah, I'm from *Spiegel Spezial*. We're doing a big rave feature. So I'm taking a survey about drugs and drug consumption.'

Us: 'My, that's very interesting. Is that fun then? What does it feel like, being a journalist, in human terms?'

Lorenz Schröter: 'Well, you know, I guess – '

'So yeah, uh,' Steffken shouted, 'Yeah, yeah, ee!' He waved away the models in front of him. He was there to snap one last front-page title photo. Laurent Garnier, captured in the posture of the late Thomas Anders, face down, so then Garnier had to gaze up from below with eyes so demonically rapt that you could see the white over the lower lid. Steffken: 'A hint of ecstasy. I always go for that when I want to really express something.'

Laurent Garnier was in a bit of a rush because he was still supposed to spin up there later. He had just put out an 'album'. He called it *30* because that expressed so much. He said he could well and truly explore himself on that album, that he was confronting an array of stylistic directions and influences, even disco and things like that. He hadn't abandoned his house roots, of course he'd integrated drum and bass, he'd worked electronica into it too. He had put up with many doubts, had lived through many doubts, now though he was quite content with himself from an artistic perspective, and even with the total result, and so on and so forth.

Steffken: 'Yeah, right, yeah!'

CHURCH OF FUN

Up front under a neon script reading *An era is past*, Jürgen Laarmann, big JL as they called him, was sitting on a little stool sober and matter-of-fact, in totally calm concentration, dictating the first final draft of his ground-breaking seven-volume work *The Laarmanizer* into the microphone of a Sony cassette recorder, clutching it in his hands and holding it close to his lips.

The working title for Volume One was *I*, yeah he'd swiped the title from Hilbig, but, as Laarmann supposedly said one time, he'd 'swiped it the right way'. Laarmann had several publishing deals in hand and didn't want to spook or startle any of the horses during the run-up. As far as planning, at least, the basic outlines of the whole project had been sketched out for some time. For him it was about tranquillity now, concentration, keeping his health in check, and maybe a sip of coke, which he actually took just then, in order to advance right afterwards: 'In 1991, still roped to the past, divided...' So Laarmann, parenthesis, had very much in mind the difference between first and last, preliminary and final, absolutely final and more or less final version and so forth, in this too he was just too professional. At that, he carried on threading things together, continuing with the continuation: 'So when I...' Laarmann paused, thought, had he not just heard that word for word in his head?

'They fall, tumble.'

This sentence appeared very true to him, was perhaps even conceivable as the motto for Volume Seven, entitled *The Millions*. Laarmann was, as he now had to admit, impressed somehow by this mental clarity of his, by the heroic moment he saw just then.

'This mental clarity here,' he thought.

Laarman leapt into the mental, or, more precisely, it leapt into him, cut to Volume 3, Book 2, Chapter 1 or 4 – that wasn't set in stone yet – sub-excursus: 'Abduction from the Gray', which gave a watertight portrayal of his hussar-and-pirate piece on the capture of *Frontpage* and its carting off to Berlin.

A little smile channelled its way visibly through Laarmann's body from deep down inside up to the interior of his forehead where it glowered silently past the expanses of the Laarmannic dura mater, and not even a single eyebrow twitched.

Grandiose.

An unbelievable affair, indeed.

A little raver girl with Mickey Mouse ears on her backpack asked for a light from the big man on his little stool. But the big man didn't have a lighter on him just then.

He shrugged his shoulders mournfully.

He begged her 'pardon'.

The word 'epoch' rose up from somewhere and got lodged somewhere. A fine mess that was. Gotta get through it now.

MEMBERS ARE JUST MEMBERS

And so it happened that –

The time will come, the Lord said, when I shall speak unto the people. And he took as his instrument the members who were there: Members of Mayday. He spoke: Look and come all, for you are all part of my kingdom that is to come, the kingdomly kingdom of ecstasy and sound. Then he gave this name to his music: Sonic Empire. And blissfully he guided the hands of his musicians at the machines.

The music thus produced, he then had preserved in sundry ways, on media of sundry sorts, on vinyl as well, of course. And the Lord resolved: This record shall rule. Then spring came and Mayday came and the following summer, and it was as the Lord had resolved, in his inscrutable counsel, this the Summer of the Sonic Empire of the Members of Mayday. So it was written, and as it was written, so it came to pass. Everything came to pass. And everything came to pass in the name of the Lord. Praised be the name of the Lord. For his name is great.

WHAT TIME IS LOVE

We went back in, and now new music was playing.

I followed the movement that started on the dance floor, and felt a pull, and when it pulled me, I found myself led to my own very own place. And only then did I realize I'd started walking in rhythm and bobbing and actually dancing. The music there was especially loud and clear, in a special area of sound no more than a few metres in circumference. Individuals had gathered there who were particularly receptive to musicospatial effects. The tone-by-tone hyper-precision of each discrete tone, and at the same time the enormity of the music's sonic intactness. Totally dope. At that moment, THE place to dance.

I danced along and these accompanying, simultaneous reflections didn't bug me. Fact: this is why you go out. Because sometimes you just have to hear music LIKE THIS, because the sounds were so sound, that and that alone was why. Roaring loud, hyper-clear. Because then you understand why they do it, why people keep going along with it, why you always want to be there, etc. etc. Jubilantly I thought the thinking of this thought. And I danced along.

Then I saw the girl from before, the one with the little fur, and I was overjoyed and at the same time horrified. I had forgotten in the intervening hours how close we had come before, furtively, without recognizing it.

I saw she was thinking something similar and was also a bit abashed. And the new understanding now established was: keep dancing like you barely know each other. Mutual interchange of movements and spaces as if the other were utterly free of any anticipation of a response. As if the immediate self-constituting togetherness had spontaneously arisen from the ever-new moment of bodily movements in thrall to nothing but the music and its movement, away from each other, towards each other, on our own, for her, for me and her, and her for herself and her for me.

So I was in love. Insanity. I didn't even know what she looked like, really. I looked at her little fur, I looked her in the face, and our eyes met and we had to laugh. No point. Or rather, yes. A point, but just a slight one, just now, nothing more. OK.

Then I thought: in parting, when she intentionally –

What had just happened, there must have been a rhythm to it. Because now all at once there came a break. And it exploded into an unbelievably thick electro-beat, and the applause was frenetic, and everyone threw themselves into dancing. You practically got hurled upward and battered by the bright, choppy party-frequency sensations and their rhythmic contrast, like a compositional element, to the offbeat pounding – an outright storm of musical bliss.

What kind of track was this, really?

I looked at the DJ stand and I saw Westbam there. Got it. The feeling of consonance overwhelmed me and I was absolutely blessed. Effacement, thank you. Once more, while I danced, I had the most lucid thoughts about a theory of critique.

'Isn't this madness?!' I said, close now to the chick with the little fur. And she nodded vigorously, obviously she too was in the middle of something, and she said, 'Exactly, exactly!'

Then it hit me: that's right, this was how the year started, at the New Year's Eve party at E-Werk, when Westbam opened to our enormous surprise with that old KLF banger 'What Time is Love.' How unbelievably cool that was at that moment, on the very first night of the year. How we danced there. Names, glances, thought cascades.

Then I walked up to the cutie pie, to say my goodbyes, and she hugged me. Total exchange of warmth. She said her name was Andrea. And she kissed me on the forehead. Everything brutally sweet.

I walked through the dancers towards the DJ booth.

STONED, DRUNK, AND WRANGLED
NAKED INTO SEX

I thought: Good. Yeah, that too.

But not to start with, not first of all.

I thought of Ulf Poschardt and his book *DJ Culture*. What is completely absent there is the real PRAXIS, the culture and art and craft of the act of mixing and phrasing, of cutting and scratching.

Culture begins at home with the cultivation of artistry in the true craft of making ONE music with two different turntables spinning at the same time.

How do you learn this lovely old craft?

Like you learn most things, pal, plain and simple, watch and imitate. When we say watch, we're talking here about close observation of what is likely the most strenuous mental activity of all: LISTENING.

You observe the activity of apprehension and calculation through the external expressions of what you can of course not observe directly: the other's brain.

How do you watch?

In the case of that exceptionally inward concentration on the music the so-called headphones convey to the brain, the face becomes a mirror transporting abstract auditory activity from the interior of the brain outward, where it is assigned to gestural actions which themselves possess a mirror-like clarity.

And so you can see what the listener thinks and consequently, next step, what he DOES.

What does the DJ do? Soon he will touch one of the turntables and do something there, with the record, with the tone arm, with the speed selector.

Does the new piece actually click?

While the music runs loud through the loudspeaker, what may be the next disc is lying on the second turntable, and the DJ is listening through the headphones to the music recorded on that record in several spots at the beginning, middle, and end, to see whether the track really is as he remembers it, whether it is the same as he thought it was when he was digging through the records in the record crate, whether it works with the piece already playing.

Result: the DJ takes the record off. He turns around and slips it back into its sleeve. What record was that? What relationship existed between the record now playing and the one just set aside? What relationship struck the DJ as dispensable given the present situation of the party?

He takes out a new record, puts it on, and listens again. He approves.

What record does he approve of? What does this record offer vis-à-vis the record set aside and the one that is currently playing? Observations of this kind yield clear reference points about the principles of consonance that the DJ aims to follow when changing records.

Perhaps – and this is the most banal case of all – he has decided for or against the continuation of the tempo; or to unite the tracks according to the analogous emotional values the different sounds have called up; or maybe he found it quite simply too boring to incorporate a totally pregnant individual sound from the first record into the second one. He has decided to maintain or discontinue the hysterical energy absorbed from the crowd, and the arousal level at this very moment may better be heightened and refined through a music-ludic practical joke than through the simple propagation of the already thriving and collectively cheered rhythm-pumping-mechanism.

And so he interrupts the showstopper dead in the middle.

Now what happens?

The DJ looks.

People watch how the DJ takes in and interprets the reaction of the public. Are people into it? Was this an error? Do things turn out differently on the dance floor from the way they appeared earlier, as pure abstraction, through the headphones and in the expansion of the concept through anticipation?

This calls for urgency.

The people are antsy. There's clearly been a misreading of the multiple dimensions of the transitory rules governing the public's reaction that are here and now momentarily in force.

In the production of an artwork that arises processually, such as the ephemeral art the DJ's craft engenders over several hours in a night, there is virtually no mistake that an apposite corrective manoeuvre cannot address or even – of course, this is the ideal situation, and in the work of the true masters, it is far from uncommon – reconfigure as a preliminary of a *new* new correctness centred around the very same mistake. But the right thing has to actually happen, and fast.

So what?

The DJ reaches for a record, throws it on the turntable, and hurries to match the tempo of the new record to the old one.

Pure art of attendance.

High-precision localization: the new record's beat drops in, it has to be slowed down slightly, when it first comes in, it is sort of limping ahead. And the converse.

To avoid directly emphasizing the mistake from before, the DJ makes a hard cut to prepare for a protracted mixing manoeuvre. Over and over he reaches for the speed selector to re-refine once more the fine tempo adjustments. He lets it run for several beats to see whether tempo and rhythm are now perfectly in sync.

His calculation has worked, his face reveals a sort of inner acquiescence. He places the tone arm at the beginning of a new record and –

He looks up.

The situation on the dance floor has changed during the scant twenty seconds that have passed. He jerks the perfectly pitched record off the turntable and brings his hands to his head.

Now good advice is dear.

Which record strikes him as unsuited to saving the situation, and why? He moves the record to the very front of the crate to play it next, to keep an eye on it.

In the blink of an eye, the word eye is meant literally here, salvation comes to him in the form of an inspiration. He bends down to the records on the floor and digs with fleet fingers through the assortment lying there. His salvation, a hit record, is lying in plain sight. But in this situation, resorting to it is anything but a hit, it's a defence manoeuvre, gutlessness. In this place, the commonplace will be nothing better than common, the commonness of the commonplace uncommonly out of place. The hit would conceal a covert cry for help, and would have ruined him and the entire situation in a way that would most likely be extremely difficult to correct.

With the new record, the DJ is on his feet again. A glance out into the public confirms his choice. Even if his first assessment of the crowd's reaction was erroneous, now he's got them tense, expectant: What's he doing? Where's he going? How, why, what for?

The new record is lying on the platter. No more pitch riding, a super-rough scratch, the collective of dancers recognizes it, responds with a shout. One dancer's shouting is sufficient to represent universal accord in this newfound eagerness. Ten recognize the next scratch, more than a hundred the following one, and they shout their praises. Cut.

The new record spins.

No-one saw this coming.

Not even the DJ.

Jubilation, shouting, a further level of all-embracing excitement.

The truly new is unforeseeable, that is the whole joke. To anyone. Even to the DJ himself. This is what distinguishes a DJ from a guy who spins records – whether dull or artfully sophisticated, underground, trashy-slummy-cynical, cut-rate-professional, doesn't matter which.

This praxis, people, this craft, this receptivity and reaction time, listening in, mixing, ordering, and rejecting, primacy of reflex, primacy of simultaneous reflection, the vision of a real departure in terms of practical implementation, the party that becomes the experience of many individuals among many others, this binding, in other words, of craft and the aesthetically novel occurrence, all this is what we will now denominate: DJ CULTURE.

We walked to the bar and talked about it. This moment of crisis and salvation.

Then I thought –

And right away I wanted –

But then it struck me –

Yeah, that was cool.

And in this way, amid the immediate experience of the thing, and even in the wake of it, in many isolated conversations, a kind of imaginary, retrospective holistic-apprehension-organ constitutes itself for the reception of the newly born and already irrevocably elapsed artwork.

This too is the locus of the mad mythos of this art.

Now the plot treads forward in big quick steps.

PROFESSOR TAUB-KARCHER: THE DARK SEQUENCE

We were standing in front of the big door.

We were supposed to leave now, to take off right away for somewhere where the light was different, and we had to, like, sit down there somewhere, and there was something we like absolutely were not supposed to do and then something else we should –

And suddenly that went just a bit too far, and I was like: 'Excuse me?'

And Professor Taub-Karcher, whose stunningly correct idea of music, in terms of form, structure, plausibility, a certain groove, a lightness and logic, which –

BIG FUN DRESDEN

'You heard of that?'

'Nah, what is it?'

'Gotta be something in Dresden, right, or...?'

'Probably.'

'I saw that somewhere. I must have read it, maybe in

the bathroom or something.'

And like me after the last night at Objekt, nah that was the night before, when we were sitting around the table with Hardy at the after-hours, all totally chill actually or like, right, the one guy, anyway, and I then stood up all of a sudden in a total panic and went upstairs like I had lost my mind, and there – my goodness. How can a thing like that happen?

And at Pulverturm, with Mate behind the DJ booth, where we were crawling around on the floor and wallowing in the muck all night or morning – or whatever part of the day it was. – To make things worse, I had my white jeans on, so everyone could tell.

Then the one time, when we woke up at Marc's and the cat had just had kittens. Little girl kittens, maybe. And at first I thought they were dead birds.

'Do tell.'

And in Zell am See, at Rave on Snow, at the after-hours, totally fucked grim scene, and this one dude asked me:
  'You want?'
And he held out a bottle of poppers to me. And I had taken something just before and was tripping, and adding that on top would have been a bit too heavy, I was already well fucked up on all the other shit. But finally I sucked it up and inhaled the vapours from the bottle and actually that was the first time I really got the popper high. Super cool and super fucked up too, obviously.

Like in Frankfurt on the Oder, not long back, when I

went into this shop and heard the music and right off was like: Whoa! For me the place was wonderful, enchanting, thanks to the drugs.

Cool!

And I had this dumb Munich cliché in my head: Music is the only drug. And I thought, yeah, sure, but also music isn't a drug, and it's also not the only one. Best to say, maybe: Music is the basic drug.

And Pata says to me: Here. So he gave me one of these superstar wonder-pills. And I accidentally just downed the whole thing, no limits, right. Everyone, horrified: Did you take the WHOLE thing? Yeah, sorry, why not?

Later, swimming, at night, at this gravel pit. The crazy ones, who scared us with their crazy drawings. And later still, next to Anki's car, with that dope tape, and then in the morning we lay there for hours on the pile of rubble in the P1 car park. And for a while nobody wanted to go home.

Like at this dress-up orgy at Alcatraz where Max was standing with a wig on his head. Or what was the deal? Who told that story?

And how later I drove all over the city with Woody to fetch some turntables. We needed two turntables right away, urgently. It took us a couple of hours. What the fuck. Then Woody played, and I lay there with the others on the bed and dozed off, totally cool.

EXPERIMENTS WITH THE VOWEL A

Then we were standing in front of the big door. It opened, and we walked in. All at once I was worried that I would look too grubby.

I said: 'I just like being with you.'

The clouds high over our heads roiled and rolled down over us in laser green. And the illuminated faces turned up towards them, astonished, amid the swaying and staggering.

I stumbled, almost tripped, almost caught myself, caught myself.

What we say and think, what we thought, before this time –

WORLD OF CHICKS

Then there were two standing there, joined in a kiss, sunken into each other, together.

And since we were down, we got down...

   Sun,
   sex-desperation,
   hot heat.

II

SUN BOOBS HAMMER

'Do you feel all right?'

We stumbled up and tumbled out. Goddamn it's bright out here, or have I got something in my eye? What's going on? What's up!

Is something there? Something, maybe, possibly? What?

What! Come again?

The eyes are blind, the eyelashes close.

Bright white: sun.

My God, is it bright here.

UNCONFUSED

The sun shone down with its atomic light over just and unjust alike, shone and bored into the eyes of all, illuminated each of them deep down to their hearts.

The blood rushes darkly inside, flushes through the lungs, quickly refreshes itself, and the heart pulls it away again, pumps it out bright red in the stamping tempo of life – ba-doom, ba-doom – through the cells all over the body hungering for oxygen.

And everyone the sun touched said: Dude, man, cut off the lights, good God is it bright here. And they pawed at their pockets, roared and trembled like rockets, but did not find the sunglasses they yearned for.

One guy standing by the bouncer said: 'You could make a mint here selling single-use sunglasses.' He started running down the figures – wholesale price, retail price, sponsoring, blablabla – murmured, jabbering the way people jabber on to no-one in particular, not caring if he communicated anything. Until finally the bouncer gets flustered and tells him off: 'How 'bout you save that shit for your hairdresser.'

Then the up-and-coming single-use-sunglasses-entrepreneur gives him a stupid look.

'Enough with the stupid look, beat it.'

Reeling and stumbling they all come up, one after the other, shut their eyes and moan and groan, cavil and clamour, grumble and grouse.

Yeah, that's it.

And the sun heats faces already hot and heated from partying, heats the moisture in their ratty clothing, their back and legs, their knees and head.

Where are we headed then?

Fugo.

Or Fortuna.

Labor.

Oberpframmern.

Already?

To see Tommy, Kerstin, Mate, Bill.

To see Angela, or Roberto, nah: to the hotel.

When's it gonna be dark again?

Maybe nice to sit down first.

Good idea.

It's midday, not yet midday. The church bells toll. Very slowly, a bulky car drives by.

The road is broad, the road is empty.

An oldish lady with stringy hair poking out from under a dusty hot pink cartwheel hat looks from the passenger seat over towards the pavement. She looks up into the poplars, leans left. Her lips move, the entire part of upper head moves, actually. The driver nods, points in front of him, now he says, 'Look.' The woman looks right again. Then she says the word 'mole'.

Then the car vanishes.

In front of the club: in grouplets and groups the burn-outs are camped out on the ground. They are lying in the warm sun and letting themselves dry out and roast.

The June sun. Slowly it glows hot and hotter, pounds and pulsates, and thus sends more and more light down to the earth. Crazy crazy.

Pigeon One: 'Supposedly this is the hottest day of the year.'

'Really?' says Pigeon Two and nods and pecks.

'Yeah, I heard that from the linden blossom aroma super early this morning.'

'Say what? It chatted you up then, huh? How nice.'

Beate, call her 'Beatrice' per her request, stands in the doorway, closes her eyes, pulls her sunglasses from her shirt's scoop neck, puts them on, and takes a deep breath. She turns left. Rolli's there sitting on a barstool, leaning against the wall, head thrown back and crooked, mouth ajar, dozing.

Beate: 'Tell me, Rolli – '

Tobi: 'Tell me? Can't you see he's asleep?'

Beate: 'He's asleep? What's he sleeping for? Did Robert already go?'

'Robert who?'

Toby lights a smoke and offers one to Beate. She thanks him, declines, sways softly on away. The men at the door make detailed observations about her figure and her stride as seen from behind, and look at each other a little nervous and amused.

What can you say about that?

Nothing, they grunt and spit and grope themselves.

'About that time,' one of them says, hours later.

After a long pause, another: 'Ya think?'

And then another: 'Maybe, maybe not.'

Zille laughed, pulled out her notepad.

'Whatcha writing down there,' said Sue, the other tall woman.

'What's with the Berlin accent?' Zille answered. 'This is Munich.'

'Like I care.'

Sue turned to the twitcher on his way out of the club twitching twitchily to the beat of a music in his head that he alone could hear. Bug-eyed, he looked the sun in its face and said to himself, 'Man, that is dope.'

Sue: 'Babe, give me a cigarette real quick please.'

The loco: 'What'd you say?'

'A cigarette!'

'A cigarette? Ah, right, got it. Wait a sec, sorry, I'll just ask the – '

'Sure thing, sweetie, that's cool.'

'Huh?'

Sue, softly, to Zille: 'Check this one out!'

Zille: 'I know.'

So the loco twitches resolutely towards the group gathered around Carsten, leans down to a blond dude with long locks dressed in leather. This guy looks up, now you can see his light blue Andy Warhol shirt with the horizontal white stripes, he beams. Paws his chest, right pocket, left pocket, behind, inside, outside, rear end, finds the box of smokes, pulls one out, and gives it to the twitcher – while talking the whole time, like nothing was happening, with Carsten, all quite gracious, almost old-fashioned, like a Christmas tree angel, cool.

The twitcher says thanks and heads back towards the door on the hunt for Sue.

Professor Taub-Karcher: 'Maybe now we should take a little something again, nice and easy. What do you think?'

Sue: 'Good idea, I'll have another beer.'

'Sue, look, the loco.'

Sue spreads her arms, the loco laughs and steadies himself against her a moment. She lifts up the cigarette she's already smoking to show it to him, but she's grateful and happy to take the one he has acquired on her behalf, and now she shows him breezily how she sticks it in her hair behind her ear, as a reserve. The loco twitches blissfully away. The cigarette drops to the floor. The professor picks it up.

Horns honking, a Turkish wedding party drives past, maybe. The cars roll forth in long columns, the horn-concert-terrorism blasts in manifold tones. White garlands, flower bouquets, shiny polished carriages. In black outfits, the black-haired men sit there unmoving.

What's the noise about? What are the images about?

Anki: 'The bride's got on a white dress, she's got a white wreath in her hair, she's even got a white veil over her face.'

'I didn't see that.'

'I did.'

Sylvie: 'For me to ever get married, hee hee hee – '

Sophie: 'When I think of marriage, I actually imagine something really beautiful.'

Pia: 'For me, the guy's gotta have money, like real money. Old money, obviously, presence, manners, and a sense of craziness. Nothing against love, mind you.'

As she talks, Pia rhythmically opens, closes, and opens her legs. She's mounted on a second barstool taken from the club and brought outside. The aperture is aimed towards Bouchti. Bouchti has to make like he doesn't notice anything so Pia will keep going. Pia is talking louder and louder. In the meantime, Sylvie and Sophie have been transformed into extras. The initial audience has now become a merely ostensible audience, while Pia's bravura performance is addressed to all members of the masculine race here assembled. Dope. Pia's got on a pair of faded-blue and bright-white acid washed jeans all scuffed up in the front.

If you do what you want and inadvertently take a peek, you faint right there on the spot.

Here Bill comes reeling, leaning on Olaf and Jerome, hacked up from the gorge of the night before, the glorious banner of BABALU lofty above him, adornment and honorific.

Bill sees Pia, growls: 'Pia!'

Pia pauses, gets down from the barstool, walks over to Bill. She's in one of those grand old alcoholic matrimonies from the 1950s. America, Technicolor, melodrama. Lovingly she makes loving gestures to Bill, full of love and tenderness for the drunk.

Bill growls: 'Come here, you slut, do the – '

Pia holds Bill's mouth closed with her hand, then replaces the hand with her mouth, in this way quieting Bill down. Pia kisses Bill with everything now, right there in front of everyone. Listless, Bill lets what's happening happen, observes how the event grades into real lust and lust into love.

Bill whispers something into Pia's ear and nibbles a bit on the little lobe hanging down from the ear. He laps the inside of the seashell, tastes salt, night, nicotine, and urine.

They lie in bed. They're breathing heavily now.

They lie in total silence.

They smoke.

They laugh.

She sees them.

She sees them, so beautiful, so so beautiful now that almost –

Olaf, nearly as drunk as Bill: 'Get me to my car! I'll drive youse home.'

Gazes wander, find Olaf, and turn back.

The paterfamilias at the McDonald's ice cream stand a few steps to the left observes these gazes with concern, how the notion flickers through the eyes of his maybe eight- or nine-year-old daughter that she has – hopefully finally ASAP please – her own life right before her eyes, she figures this out right away, observing this dramatization of the forbidden.

She jumps up and twitches, kicks up her legs, bobs and weaves like a decapitated chicken.

'Isabelle!' shouts the father, his overly stern tone surprises him, but at the same time he jerks more sternly still at the red bow over his daughter's bottom.

The mother says to the father, 'Don't be so dramatic, dear,' and to rebuff him, pats the daughter on her daughterly hair, which is long and lush like wild chives.

Sunday morning, Leopoldstrasse, just before eleven: Do you know where your daughter is?

Isabelle scurries off, stops in front of Olaf, tugs at the front of her little dress, and screeches: 'I'm Isabelle, who are you?'

Olaf mimics her tone of voice: 'With or without an E at the end?'

'With, of course. And you?'

'I'm Olaf.'

'Olaf.'

'Yeah, I'm your nasty Uncle Olaf. Come sit on my lap, little girl, I've got something pretty to show you.'

Isabelle with an E, appalled, confused: 'You're drunk!' She punches Olaf in the belly, claws at his arms, shrieks loud and strident. Simultaneous screaming from each of the parents, the mother screams, the father screams.

The mother jogs over. She already knows what the daughter's up to. She looks Uncle Olaf in the face and is horrified. She is afraid for herself.

Curses back at the cursing father.

Now they are standing there holding their stupid Sunday ice creams in their stupid hands.

Silence.

No-one says anything.

Everyone offends everyone.

Shaw family comes over. Polite greetings from person to person, the usual niceties amicably exchanged.

Yeah.

Nah.

True.

Of course.

Right.

For sure.

OK, OK.

Mrs Shaw, Mr Shaw, and little Miss Shaw vanish.

Again, immediately: silence, wordlessness, and intensive activation of wicked thoughts.

Olaf: 'Keep it up. You'll see what's what soon enough.'

The Irish approach as a growling horde. They'd already beat a few Englishmen to a pulp at Münchner Freiheit.

Now they want more, with someone here, if possible, thanks.

Nobody here wants to throw down? You think you're better than us, then? You trying to put us down? What gives?

The Irish stomp quick and nasty with boots and hurrahs on the kidneys of a few poor ravers. Little joke. Bouchti negotiates with the leader. A case of beer is found and brought out. Hacki sets down the crate, pops the caps off with his lighter, and toasts with the Irish.

'Cheers.'

The Irish take their beers and settle down. They toast each other, fraternize with the ravers. The pizzeria waiter groans. Norbert gives his blessing. He's got on white gloves, red shoes, a cardinal red robe.

That night I dreamt I was hidden in a strange place, in an unknown city. I was in a completely different story.

Sigi steps on the scene, screams, roars. The mood is tip-top.

Susi, Sassy, Caro, Kathi: a car full of chicks, it's Susi's big body Benz, a straight-up beater, dark blue. Kathi's driving. The car is giving off smoke. They're up on the pavement, Kathi weaves through the people, pulls right up to the door, and gets out.

'Woody! Let's go! Come on!'

Tom: 'Come on!'

Sigi: 'Come on!'

Sigi grabs his throat like he's thirsty and says: 'Thirsty!'

Tom pleads with Tobi, who bends down to the right rear window next to where Susi's sitting. She hands him something. They talk.

The new plan is: Kraftwerk, Pulverturm, then this open air thing that's going on all day somewhere past Riem.

So who's playing there? Who's putting the thing on?

The information is altogether a bit confused and scanty.

Initial suggestions from all sides that just maybe right here right now an intentional departure could possibly get slowly underway or at least perhaps some indication of said departure might come into view, unless all this is just a delusion, which is not in the least bit less possible.

At the moment, Robert is still going with his Egyptian king routine. He's got a falconer with him, and he gives him directions in something, Egyptian, maybe. Just so happens Robert speaks many different languages. He tells the falconer to quiet down a bit, then tenses his bow. An arrow flies forth. In German, Robert tells the spectators this is an ancient hunting ritual in which the gazelles and other beasts of the steppe were killed, but only in appearance – Robert takes another arrow out of his quiver, sets it, and tenses the bow – to receive the grace of the gods, now he says quite softly, just for today. He shoots the arrow, announces the animal has been hit, his mission fulfilled.

He picks up a javelin off the ground and steps forward in a javelin thrower pose. This is the javelin throw, an Olympic event, he's in Athens, the falconer is his masseur. Now it's time for the all-important third attempt. He starts in the name of all his relatives, dedicates this final throw to everyone he knows. All the people he knows from Yugoslavia, from Pl, from Reitschule and from Partysanen, they must wish him luck for his great performance.

A bit louder, please. A bit more enthusiasm. Robert lets the javelin sink, stands there like a pop star, allows the others to applaud him. The javelin is now a microphone in a microphone stand, Robert is a rapper from the Wu Tang Clan. He's rapping in heavy rhythmical chunks, rapping in imaginary Hispano, in international crazy American slang, and in the midst of it telling his public the story of the multi-coloured wild dog.

And then – and then –

Robert throws the microphone to the falconer, has to rush behind his turntables. Extreme mixing, extreme scratching, above all ultra-extreme extreme headphoning. He takes the last record from the platter, briefly mimics a discus thrower, he could automatically transition into that from here, he lets the record sail off smoothly into the air and turns to Sigi.

'Sigi, now!'

Sigi doesn't react. Robert picks the javelin back up, does a bit of extreme sex dancing in the guise of a woman, strokes the shiny metallic tube on the stage at the cheap disco, half-naked in the cage, lit up by the spotlights. 'For you I'm nothing but a cheap sex object!' Robert shouts. All he's looking for, he says, is a little bit of love, like everyone, like all of us.

He takes the hand of the unknown woman standing next to him and squeezes it between his legs. The woman doesn't even get offended, she just says drily, 'You're off your rocker, old timer,' pulls back her hand, and slaps him.

Robert: 'Come on, babe, not in front of all the people here. Please.'

Sigi tugs his T-shirt out of the front of his trousers, pulls it up over his heart side, and cries, elbows over his head: 'Now!'

He turns to the girls and says: 'Show us your tits!'

Kerstin walks up to Sigi, lifts up her boobs, jiggles and comes closer and closer and asks: 'Like this, Sigi?'

Sigi pulls away. Walks off: 'Show us your tits!'

All of a sudden looks totally consternated.

A dark-skinned girl, shirt black over the radiance of her brown flesh, reaches one hand back as far as she can towards the middle of her back, scratches the hollow of her back, real slow please, thanks.

Bewilderment.

The girl turns slightly from one side to the other, she's got her hair cut in a black pageboy, freshly combed, dried, polished, she is maximally brutally cute.

'Where's the deal with that chick there?' Sigi says to Martina, 'How come I don't know her? You know her?'

Martina: 'Where am I supposed to know her from?'

Sigi: 'You don't think she's hot?'

'Yeah, she's hot all right.'

'Come on, let's snap her up.'

They go slowly in the chick's direction, couple steps, Sigi: 'No, mistake, stop.' They walk back.

Sigi, now louder, to the chick: 'Hey sweetheart! Come over here!'

She turns around and laughs and at the same time acts peeved, but not too much, this is a beautiful woman we're talking about here.

She says: 'What kind of tosser are you? Come over here yourself if you feel like it.'

Sigi: 'Nah, sorry, you're right. It was just a joke. For real though: come here a second! I can't leave. I got a really important question for you though.'

'What kind of question?'

'Just come here a second, please. I can only tell you over here.'

The beautiful woman stands up to full height, bends over, grabs her clutch bag, stands back up, and turns around. Then she stops short for a moment. She's showing what she's got, she smiles, Sigi nods to her. Then she leaves.

Just a few steps, but they last.

She walks off in beauty-slow-mo, and everything turns towards her. She's transformed into the goddess such-and-such. She's feeling shrewd, she's shrewder than she thinks, she feels her body inwardly suffused with this immense inward thing, with a power that surges through her, that has come down to her from she knows not where. She sees herself in this moment as the centre and dwelling place and temple of a beautiful soul, and she sees how the whole world sees this, hails it, praises it, and rejoices. As she walks, she naturally averts her eyes to the sides a bit and to the floor, so others can look at her in peace.

Then, after a few steps, she makes her way over to Sigi, elated by all this, by the whole cool collective looking-and-showing act.

She stops in front of Sigi, laughs.

Sigi: 'Closer!'

'What do you mean, closer?'

'You gotta come closer, otherwise I can't tell you.'

'How come? Is this OK?'

Sigi whispers, very softly, very close to her cheek: 'You are one super-hot chick. So what's up?'

'Sorry, what's the question?'

'The question is: What brings you here? Where do we go next? Why don't I know you?'

Sigi lifts his right arm, cocks it back, and gives the beauty the opportunity to try out leaning in on him. She goes along with it and laughs. Sigi squeezes her brashly, almost a bit too tenderly, briefly lets loose his obvious hunger for sex, then goes right back to being playful. She leans into him, takes a breath, now she's got his scent.

Sigi's a nice guy.

The beauty is a super-hot young woman.

Nothing's yet been decided.

Water emerges through the skin, to cool the system and to liven you up. It's wet, it's hot and it's comfortable to sweat like this all over, skin grazing against skin. The water flows. The skin heats up.

Noon has now found its routine.

No-one's moving.

No-one else.

Nothing.

Nothing and no-one and nobody is now moving.

'You expect –

well no wonder –

something wonderful, though!'

Anne is reading an advert for Philips in *Petra*. It's about cellulite.

'Or should we say *cellulitis*, like Harald Schmidt would say,' says Anne. She has written a so-called culture piece for *Petra* about a classic culture theme: girl bands, Die Braut Haut ins Auge, major stuff. For five years or so this article has had to be rewritten at least once a year by an aspiring female Communications or Cultural Studies student and republished in one of these culture rags. Otherwise the world would just up and stop spinning. Isn't that so?

At the Tank: Can you please take that down. But of course. Not an issue, as they say. The culture press, then, for example:

Marie Claire, Allegra, Maxi, Max,
Frauen Magazin, Cosmopolitan, Prima Carina,
Für Sie, Men's Health, Haar Scharf, Madame,
Vogue, Coupé, Bellevue, Brigitte,
Tina, Yoyo, Annabelle, Emanuelle, Isabelle,
Elle, Praline, Anne.

Typical: Anne rings up some foreign writer, some editor or professor, you can just chat up anyone that way, and then, in the first twenty seconds, she assaults these so-called men of letters by uttering the word 'clitoris' straight into their ears. Just like that, doesn't mean anything, it's just a word. The word 'clitoris'.

It has an effect.

How so? What kind of effect?

Weird. Totally gaga.

'Clitoris'. It's just a little teensy weensy ticklish little soundlet that the foreign woman implants via oral administration into the head of a foreign man via telephone.

Freedom. Cool.

Asinine. Bullshit. Thanks a lot.

Still, the editors are browbeaten and they print whatever Anne and the other Anne, her friend, write. Even now the two Annes are, by the by, gathering material for their amusing little newspaper column, which appears once a week on the Munich Culture page of the *Süddeutsche Zeitung* page with the cool title *Kobold*. For like four or five months the two Annes have been into music and going out, too, and drinking and Luhmann and drugs and all the other stuff that goes along with that

109

whole spectrum of all the so-called 'electronic aspects of life' *Kobold* talks about.

Anne: 'For me *Kobold* is a way of playing.'

The other Anne: 'We are testing out totally new, untried ways of writing.'

Anne: 'People are either totally into it or they think it's totally stupid. Nothing in between. That's cool, though.'

Anne tells the other Anne about London. She's researching an article about ketamine. She just got back yesterday. She's got to see whether she can maybe line up a little ketamine in Munich, it's gotta be possible to set up a ketamine connection real quick on a beautiful Sunday like this one. Maybe she'll drink a little bubbly, then just call up someone she doesn't know.

Something always works out.

Firm, the heat hangs there, there shines the sun, not a single person moves from the spot in such weather. And the treetops of the poplars sway soft and slow above.

Further off, hidden, on the other side of the street, a window casts reflections, and behind it: the police. There are two younger guys up there in jeans and white T-shirts, weapons dangling down in holsters under their armpits: that's the international cool criminal style.

Someone's filming, taking photos, they fool around with a directional mic. They take notes. Gather names, observations. Not much is going on, that's normal at this time. It's something about the falconer, but you can just barely hear.

'Take that with you.'

The falconer moves self-assured in Robert's fidgeting shadow. His eyes wander. He's on the lookout for his courier, who took off for Wiesbaden this morning. He was supposed to be back a long time ago. Something's up. Maybe something really is up.

The falconer studies the scene: How long should he keep waiting?

The falconer's keeping it extremely cool. The calculation is like so: Experience says getting suspicious, reacting reactively to potential dangers, getting ahead of yourself, is worse than just waiting, in danger of a possible double-cross.

The falconer waits.

The falconer gives Robert a sign and goes towards the door, goes slowly inside, down into the club.

'Get a move on, to the office!'

The brown tablets apparently have heroin mixed in with them, that's what someone said.

Who says?

Anyway the yellow ones were better. They were just as good as – I quote – 'before'.

What's that supposed to mean? What kind of unadulterated absolute horseshit is that?

Besides, the yellow ones are gone.

Shit? Really?

I'm gonna handle it.

Downstairs in the former stables, all at once, the lights come up for cleaning.

Miss Katharina enters the women's toilets and hurries back out, because she's sensed the heat of sexual intercourse inside. She is a mannered older lady of Italian origin who for more than twenty years has been employed in the service of this place, she's stayed with it while tenants and owners have come and gone. She opens the door to the men's toilets, water rushes out towards her. She shuts the door again. Miss Katharina sets down her bucket and walks back through the narrow, rubbish-packed hallway towards the office.

As she walks, she makes a bit of noise, so the people in the office know she's there. Whispers filter out from the office.

In the office the cocaine, laid out in lines across a record, is briefly, temporarily tucked, with a practised sweep of the hand, in among the accounts folders on the shelf. Miss Katharina sees four, five, maybe six faces crowded together. The office is a room of one and a half or two metres square at most.

Miss Katharina makes a door-locking motion with her hand. 'Got to lock up. Closing time.' From inside comes grunted acquiescence, the door closes again. Without another word, the record with the cocaine makes its rounds. One person declines, the rest are down.

Sniff and snort.

Snuffle and grunt.

Hock, hiss, harrumph.

Smoking and walking.

'See ya, Miss Katharina. Thanks.'

Later it was supposed to be shown –
    but who can speak here of should, of ought, of decree? –
    that –

Yeah, the office is bugged. And it would be so nice to act like we knew that just now. But, as it happens, we don't.

We don't know the telephone has been tapped here for some time, at the other clubs, at the Boy, at everyone's houses. Nor, hard as it may be to believe, do we know that from inside the construction trailer parked purposelessly for months on end on the street right across

112

from the club on all the major days – so every Thursday, Friday, Saturday, and Sunday morning, and of course every Sunday afternoon, when the gay-T-dance begins, yes indeed – one and all have been photographed and videotaped umpteen times and are being photographed again every day, up to and including today.

You don't ever really think you're so important just because of that little bit of fun, that little bit of excess you get into at night. And yet you hear the noise that comes along with it, maybe lately you've even been hearing it a little too loud. The stupid *tz*, the stupid *AZ*, the stupid *SZ*: every one of them is writing about it.

Just leave us be, you dipshits.

They don't even think about it.

And then the film teams move in, from TV whatever, from Mag X and zine Y, with their pathetic cameras and cameramen, their cute dumb editors, the absolutely dullest genus of people known on earth, they act all important, every time you turn around they're like 'Roll.'

Stay home. Tape somewhere else. Go away.

We hate you.

They just can't get it. They think they're important, they quite earnestly believe, as in the early days of TV, that everyone is automatically happy for some stupid camera to point at them and disrupt their life. They feel like society has truly tasked them with a truly true task.

We've all talked to them, too much. Whoever comes from TV, whoever works for TV, is dumb, there's no fixing it, no fixing it at all, dumb down to the depths of their pus-soaked skulls, conceited and insolent, dumb as a rock, as the dumbest of rocks, some of them maybe even dumber than a rock.

Yeah? Is that so? You don't say?

Yeah, that's so.

113

Blessed be, on the other hand, our police.

So they had a raid planned. A loose net lay over everything, a broad net of data and metadata lay over and around everyone. And the State Criminal Police weave and cast their net calmly, persistently, without excessive zeal. For a long time now anyway, people have known more than they might like to know, more than they ought to know and more than they officially know. Given the current state of knowledge, they should act, actually they should have acted some time ago. They forfeited the freedom to exercise good judgement long ago.

But now something's happened: a mother has recently lost her very young daughter – and this is how it's supposed to be, right? So it is foretold, and so it is written in all the statutes of life – to the night and to its dark, eldritch drives. And as it happens, wouldn't you know it, the stupid mother is also Chief of the Municipal Office for Law and Order. Ever since then, there's been pressure from the authorities, and hysteria on the part of the politicians.

A beautiful thing, *en passant*: women in positions of power, mothers in ministerial posts. What you get with that is this pincer-tone, this peculiar caring-idiocy, a rage for prescriptions and childrearing impressed onto public life. It's imperative to treat the entire world like a child who doesn't know what's good for him, for the rest of the world, for anyone. Mothers do know, and they shout it in public and express their voice with their vote. A normal person, you automatically turn the volume down. Thank you, ministerial mothers, women in politics.

At first, the cops remain quiet. There's an order to listen and learn, everyone involved knows it, they've practised

114

calmly for years with the requisite degree of reason-ableness, but now they're in a nervous, not gratuitously irritable balancing act.

The owner is rung up and summoned for a voluntary informal information-gathering chat.

You know yourself this is no good for any of us, all the stuff that keeps showing up over and over in the papers. Be reasonable, don't make any extra headaches for yourself or us. There's no reason for it. At some point the club is gonna get pinched. Unless things change.

The State Criminal Police guy is one of these official types. Munichy, bureaucratically subdued and precise, frank but not excessively demonstrative. An athlete, maybe, a mountain climber or surfer, mid, late thirties. 'A pleasure, Mr Kern, just take a seat please.' He doesn't need to say anything else, he knows a place like that isn't even thinkable, let alone viable without drugs, because he knows the guy across from him knows and knows that he knows.

And the other way around – etcetera etcetera.

A kind of reciprocity, understand.

But he makes clear that the climate of these past few weeks and the information made officially available to him in accordance with his position threaten to turn this into an even more explosive situation just now. So: Be careful, please. Get it?

Absolutely, Mr Neuener.

It makes things easier, even if things were to turn out differently, that Mr Neuener has sitting across from him a young man whom the office knows – and this is absolutely an exception for a club of this sort – takes no banned substances whatsoever himself.

This is the way things have been, for years now. That now bears unexpected fruit.

'I don't have to do a damned thing,' Wolli says, setting down a beer, 'we're calling it a day, you all can go home or you can go somewhere else, go to the English Gardens if you want, but here we're closed. Over and out.'

The intertwined vegetables lying there on the floor look up dumbfounded at the big, tall man with the bared head.

'Wolli!' one shouts.

'Yeah?'

'Please!'

'No.'

This is the ritual: end of the workday, the whole thing has got to be acted out over again from A to Z every time. With childlike joy at the simple, the simplest conceivable repetition of immutable simple rituals, all participants enact and perform all these rituals over and over again.

That's just how it goes.

So it's midday, midday on Sunday, and in Schwabing in Munich the Leopoldstrasse, venerable precursor to all Schwabing sensations, is now back in business. The shops in the vicinity of Babalu – the pizzeria, the McDonald's, and the little Chinese takeaway on the corner – are now serving their guests tranquilly. Across the street, the Roxy has filled up, the people are sitting down for breakfast, the *big brunch* as it's called, inside and out on the patio, and on the pavement, Sunday strollers from Murnau and Fürstenfeldbruck, from Straubing and Altötting wend their way forwards. It seems everyone is moving happily in herds and hordes through their lives, all over the world.

Do you understand that?

Maybe, I mean why not? On the other hand –

Just a moment. What was the question again?

116

In essence we've now reached an ideal circumstance, this extremely desirable circumstance of exhaustion and exhausted enthusiasm when at the end of the sentence you no longer know what the sentence was actually about at the beginning, back when you started the sentence in some faraway earlier –

'What were you saying?'

'Sorry, can't remember.'

'No probs, me neither.'

The last scattered denizens of Babalu sit in ever-diminishing groups of stragglers, in the interim they've crept a bit closer to the club, they're on the ground, rolling up and smoking, laughing, chatting, and dozing, and caging for drinks, constantly, please, today, now. It is seen as proper and normal and wholesome to lie on the ground where animals and children pass and vegetal life nourishes itself from below.

Mild mood, world observation.

No-one has to have to do anything anymore, that's done with, too. That's in the past now. You've survived the big adventure of the night, you've made it out again, through the night, somehow. The fear, what's it going to be like, when will it all take off, how it will turn out this time: gone, simply gone. You can hardly recall that there was a time, sometime, when the night had a beginning. And there is no more urgent or categorical need to talk everything over again, to address and discuss the big picture and the details, to question them, turn them back and forth, to postulate and reject – the thoughts and insights wander in each person in rich and manifold forms. This is a kind of vigilance concerned with society, with what it is, with the life one leads.

All that's forbidden, that goes without saying, that is

normal and totally reasonable. Even a child can understand that.

'Take me to my car! I'll drive you home!': Olaf.
   'Put on a new record, I can't listen to this BS anymore.'
   'Really? Why? It hooks me every time.'
   'Like with Kraftwerk, it's the same thing: first, at
the beginning: cool. Bumping sound, funky groove,
everything's the way you know, the way you expect, the
way it ought to be. But already BY the second track, not
even at the end, right in the middle of the second track
you're already getting impatient, already you're thinking: Yeah, OK. Cool. I know, I get it.

But they *don't* get it up there on the stupid little
stage. They are just too DULL, these gentlemen from
Kraftwerk, this is what they don't grasp: how to stretch
out your antennae and check for how the public is
feeling. They just run through their weird-ass look-
how-we're-not-moving act, it's dull and it's hollow. Wow,
incredible, a revolution: very cool, super boring. After
eight minutes the whole thing was a joke, the whole stupid Kraftwerk concert. A journey back in time, OK,
maybe, but a torture any way you slice it.

Hurry up and put a new record on, please.

But they wouldn't. It dragged on for more than two
hours, these presumptive gods with their tedious idiocy,
this music's fathers and grandfathers.

Puppet show. Dreadful.

Legendary, as they've said, as we were saying from
the very first moment.

But what was it like? What was Kraftwerk like?

Legendary, sure. A magic moment for all the writers
who then could write their laughable falsehoods from
pure –

118

Hey, now, what's that supposed to –
WHAT'S THAT SUPPOSED TO BE?!'

At that, the thing that only so slowly, well, to be honest, that's actually been completely absent here: the music.

Question being: Who had which tapes with what on them?

Who can actually get around, with what car?

And where to now?

And who with whom?

Best thing would be to keep things cool and talk it over right quick.

The talking over starts.

The talking over drags, drags on.

The talking over is still dragging on.

The great council is now in session, is still in session, in the meanwhile is growing stagnant.

It's about to start, right? Maybe.

Or maybe now?

Probably right away.

But who can do it, who really wants to know it clearly.

AND THE SAGA CONTINUES

I lie on the ground, in the grass, under trees, and it doesn't surprise me how my body rebels and lurches in gathering wild spasms that rise up from my stomach, shake me all over, gag me and make me retch. Nothing comes up, though. In the last I don't know how many hours, a few days at any rate, I haven't taken anything at all. Except for a few pills, some hash cookies, speed, and cocaine.

And so I lie there on Hell Night at Suicide, in the yard at Suicide stinking from the portaloos, under the trees in the grass, somehow next to or under the so-called Hackesche Höfe, in Mitte, as they say here, in Berlin, and I puke on the ground in front of me and I think: Now it's over. That helps.

Eventually the gagging stops, the spasms ease up, and I look calmly at the tree stump, at the branch lying crosswise in the perspective before me. Too weary to scrutinize it in greater depth, to grasp it. From behind someone comes over, asks if he can help me, and with all my strength I get real carefully back up and say in a very orderly fashion: 'No, thank you very much. I'm just going to rest for a moment here.'

Then I lie down again, motionless, eyes wide open, and sense the beating of the heart-lung-machine pumping softly inside me, gratitude, I sense life, how it courses through me, and is there, and is a blessing. How the earth cradles me. How I am lying on it, in it, so close. How my eyes close.

Images come, thoughts, a so so quiet succession. I fall. And sleep comes.

Again the white pinnacles.

Olaf and me, and the heat, and this, as they say, Ibizan light.

A certain kind of philosophy that examines forgetting, which we have smoked ourselves into slowly over the course of the morning hours, calmly, inadvertently, actually, without meaning to. It just happened.

Ommmm. You become a very old wise man, eastern or southern Mediterranean, and it doesn't bother you, quite the opposite: once more the situation has occurred, as it has so often this summer, the situation we ourselves have extolled several times now, with everything arising from and proceeding into the feeling of being totally and utterly super comfortable.

My notebook is lying between us like a plaything, and each of us notes down what happens to him, whatever strikes him as fitting. We give things special names. Things: spirit.

How we think, how the process of thinking proceeds within us. As always, we would gladly know more. Essential data is missing, facts known to man, forming part of man's knowledge, but lamentably unknown to us. Nothing new-fangled: medicine, please, neurophysiology and biochemistry, molecular bonds, processes, conditions in the interior of the atom, and so on and so forth. Might it simply be too much to ask to know all that, to have it at hand as totally run-of-the-mill knowledge twitching, quaking, and living inside you? Apparently so.

Wanting to know more then, and turning your eyes up, looking up and letting them wander far out there over the blue and shimmering silvery-sunlit surface of the sea. This other longing that tugs at all of us, a foreign violence within, a melancholy without end.

We decided to ditch the airplane we were supposed to catch some time this afternoon, and instead we split the last half-pill and went down to the pool and then after all that got tired for some reason.

Alas.

Best thing would be if at this moment we just never had to go to sleep again. Our weariness brings back the distance between us, the normal distance that exists between people. For just a moment it was gone, just a moment before. Super beautiful, the moment that had briefly been.

Madness.

Madness, basically, an asocial social situation. That's no good. When that's the deal, sleep is appropriate: everyone always does that alone. In the interior of the brain, isolated basically from everything and existing for itself, sleep is a mental act only valid and beneficial for its master and its body, and as such cannot be shared.

Well then.

The others have got up and come to the pool and now they are making a little bit of noise, jumping in and splashing around. That wakes me up. I hop in the water, too, and feel almost completely sober all at once, thanks to this bit of sleep at the edge of the pool.

The villa belongs to the guys from Frankfurt, they're the ones who invited us up here to the hills, somewhere off in the nowhere of this majestic island. Last night, this morning, rather, after the full moon party on the beach, after it was over, when was that? Around eight, maybe nine, maybe later.

Spoon had closed with 'Walking Down Madison' and 'Andromeda', kept playing them over and over and over and over, because that was the absolute last song, because the bar owner was standing there leering, and finally it was like: one more, ONE more song – so he let the track run on endlessly, kept picking the needle up at the end and bringing it back to the beginning, the shift manager didn't catch on, didn't pick up on the song's endless swaying and surging. How I worshipped him for it. Big bad wicked Spoon.

Then at some point it was finally over and done and finito, and I sat on this little wall next to the turntables and the equipment and watched everything get broken

122

down, watched how Spoon and Sven chucked their re-cords into the crates, their magic raw materials, how they talked and smoked and dealt with this and that, perfectly in tune with all the final hours of the night, the party, the many long journeys many of those pres-ent had undertaken, and now it was the morning hour. When the crazies were beating a retreat. And the lords of the day and of the daytime business return and, great, take back their reign.

I see Sven there for the first time, understand the Sven thing. How he's there like that. How I am captivat-ed, spellbound right away, nothing else to say about it. And again I find, inevitably find, as I've found so many times before: that those rumoured to be great, publicly regarded as somehow great, ARE actually a thousand times greater than all that. How the rumours, the rep, the so-called image, the public portrayal are always true.

Sven Väth, Maniac Love.

Exactly, exactly, exactly exactly exactly.

And now they're all standing there, it's time to take off, and we're standing around there, too, and the first fam-ilies show up with bag and baggage and little children's cries.

And then Sven just happens to invite us along, too, to keep partying, at their place, his place, they had rented a villa in the hills, a half-hour from here maybe, it was nice there, but only if we wanted to, yeah, gladly.

And the fact is, he doesn't even know us. He barely knows us, knows Uncle Olaf a little, basically hardly at all. And yet he just IS like this with strangers and so is the same with us. He is this king of hearts of the sav-ages who evokes savagery, draws it close, has savagely roused, aroused the hearts of so many, so delicately, somehow.

And then we're off in an open-topped Jeep chasing a convertible on snaking roads through the hills, everything green, bright, and gentle, damp-fresh, mossy, over and through and off into the island.

The wind is blowing.

And Olaf is talking away idiotically.

Behind the wheel again, yet again, sits the drug baron. We're his prisoners, don't you know.

As soon as we arrive, he's standing there at the airstrip, scraggy, sombre, lanky. Late late forties maybe.

He's there to pick us up.

Seriously? For real?

We don't really know him. Me not at all, Olaf gets him records sometimes.

When the engine cranks up in the car, the music starts up with it. And the guy starts going off about the tape, some records Olaf sent him, the party tonight, which we can't miss. A private party, on one of these so-called *fincas*, all tucked away somewhere, with punch and all.

And so he drives us into the city, and now there really is no lack of advice and wink-nudges and tricks and insider tips. A bit exhausting, the whole thing. But we're not here to have a good time, we're here to party.

In front of the little trash-pension, twenty marks per double room per night, we get out, and the drug baron drives off and waves, and I look at Olaf, slightly unnerved, and ask: 'You really know that dude from somewhere?'

'Nope. How come?'

Olaf, Wolli, Olli: the social world champion class.

Later we drive the mopeds we rented from an English

lady at the moped rental place across the road to the beach, to Salinas, walk on past the furthest bar and lie in the sun and doze.

Nice music, very good-looking people.

Partly naked, of course. I see a woman, sporty type, elegant, thin, maybe just past thirty, with splayed legs lying on her back and no pubic hair in the front. But not shaved, it's just like that naturally, crazy, you can see it clear as glass. Agitation rears its head, for the sake of politeness we had best not follow it. Agitation, in this case, means a brief, hurricane-like thundering roaring through you, a madness, a lunacy, a no-no, an upheaval that nestles cruelly and pathetically and beyond all repair in every cell in the body and rages and moans there mutely.

Then tranquillity is restored.

And with time you get slowly used to the scenery around you here, despite everything. Then the music plays, and the sun shines, the sand lies there, and we lie on it, and the sea rushes dully, in mute waves. Even the people there walk prettily in their anonymous wonderful bodies, from the bar into the sand, over the stones to the jetty, out over the jetty in the direction of the sea, and then they jump into the water.

Everything is like in *Tag am Meer*, the mood is mega-relaxed. Just right. The whole of human beauty, the seductions of which the gods yielded to with joy, rejoiced at when they were still alive, before Olympus, and near to man, once.

Dawn, hammer, doze.

No-one is helping anyone. And naturally everyone is helping everyone, somehow.

And so you felt grasped by something that was not you, and could not do this alone, could in no way produce a thing like this only for yourself, which far exceeds you as an individual: the elegant action of social systems.

Then the drug baron, whose name is actually Marc and whose main job is being a paedo, showed up at the beach, greeted everyone he could with a handshake, settled down next to us, and went on generating text again like a madman.

We talk about a number we've got planned, one we're hoping to do, with a heavy, loose dub beat, smoked out, almost reggae-ish, like a super deep low slack groove that just keeps thumping, overlaid with these tinkly poppy house piano riffs and an irrisory, lost melancholic melody of wind sounds, brass and woodwinds, an operatic spectrum, Italo-western style, the mere spectrum of sounds would be like the auditory equivalent of extra widescreen, and so on, and the piece builds up like this and when it reaches the really beautiful part: pow, break, of course – and then super soft and repulsively close, flush to your ear, real skanky, you get my voice:

'There laughs
the heart
of the paedo Dutroux –
and – mine – too.'

And then obviously after the obligatory super-short microphone pause, the jolt comes back full blast: dub-schmaltz. Sounds dope, right. Also the track's supposed to be called *Kratylos*, because it would be about the word *disgrace*, you know, and our project would be called *JR*, for Jerome and Rainald. I'm thinking of *JR* as an open, agreeably confessional child-sex-project, but Jerome doesn't know anything about that yet. Of course, you

126

wouldn't exactly just announce something that unequiv-
ocally at the beginning, you'd ease it in slowly over time,
track by track, let it emerge with increasing clarity. And
in the end the thing would turn into a child-sex-glorifi-
cation monument, a kind of Pierre et Gilles worldview
celebration, transposed into the acoustic, into the musical realm, but without the gay obsession, or with both,
one hundred per cent polymorphously perverse, so with
little girls too and all that, obviously.

It's sweet: child sex for all.

Total harmony. Beautiful children, and then everything totally cool.

Problem being: everyone I tell about the thing finds
the idea completely repulsive. The idea just doesn't catch
on. And I mean not one bit. No-one perceives the beauty
in it, the ideal that I see, the completely normal part, if
you will.

The next day, after the private punch party at the isolated clandestine so-called *finca* in the middle of who
knows where, which is actually a giant villa with multiple levels of rooms and terraces and more halls and
chimneys than you can count, with torches and fires
in every nook and cranny and masses of people all
fire-toasted and leathery and spiritually ground down
from the abundant sun and drugs over twenty or more
years in the service of the good life on the island – where
we got lost quick fast right away – and much later, on
the other side of the night, with an older French lawyer
and a few young guys who had come over especially
for this party from an eco-colony on Formentera with
a plastic bag full of pills, I wound up in a hotel in the
middle of Ibiza Town, where others were describing and
discussing everything imaginable in English, and I just

sat there agreeing agreeably with it all and felt a gentle fulfilment from the gestures or words addressed to me now and again, so that I nodded a little and said: Yeah, yeah, sure – until – Yeah, until what really? – at some point I wound up sitting alone at an outdoor table in the old city drinking coffee at the so-called Croissant Show and smoking a – and then Olaf came over, too.

'You're here?! Rad!'

On the door to our hotel room Olaf has found a note from Marc inviting us this very afternoon at such-and-such a time to a certain café in some backwater out towards the centre of the island called Santa Virtudinis or something along those lines, and also telling us to be ready for some dude we won't know but who's a good friend of Marc's and whose name was or who went by the name Salah Ben Mahrez – and so on and so forth – and now Olaf reads out this weird note, and this is the point where I say to Olaf:

'Look, all this sounds totally absurd, what could this dipshit want with us?'

Olaf: 'Some kind of courier service, probably.'

Aha. Got it. Sure. Right on.

We'll take the bill, please, thanks, and out.

Later, after a snatch of sleep in the room in the pension, where, despite constant darkness, the heat had climbed to a moist 64 degrees approx, we bought newspapers from the kiosk and we're sitting in front of Monte Sol, and I'm eating an asparagus omelette in strict accordance with the law of the land.

The *Bild-Zeitung* has let their successful editor-in-chief Larhass go. The photo shows a guy with a truculent mug, you can really see he's the type who pays 'attention to detail' as they say nowadays, whether with Harald

Juhnke's photo or face or some spot on Franzi's panties. Now one 'Geist' is supposed to be coming over from *Die Welt*, a Wolfgang Geist, supposedly. They say that's his name, you can read it right here. *Das Bild* is, understandably, growing disgusted with itself, has given the green light to a so-called 'Richter'. A kind of over-boss or over-over-boss. They say you're not even supposed to utter this Richter's name, instead you tap yourself on your double chin if one of Richter's orders comes up, as an allusion to the remarkably rotund, chubby, literally mani-fold lobulous double chin that droops down far over Richter's shirt collar.

Everything is laid out and broken down amusingly from A to Z and scrutinized down to the last litigious detail in a gigantic article in the Finance section of the *FAZ*. Springer, Kirch, Mohn, and what's the name of the family again that bought *Die Zeit*? The one with the daughter who's this legendary publisher at Fischer. All of them have their moment there, bim bam boom, the entire family. Absolutely grade-A reading material.

FAZ, how we love thee.

In the Feuilleton they discuss – *uno, dos, tres* – Ricky Martin's story *Deconspiration*, which is about Schirrmacher's committing suicide because of his Stasi entanglement. The discussion was particularly critical of so-called *ad personam* attacks. Retired Second Lieutenant Ulrich Raulff takes the floor in *SZ Magazin*, which is supposed to be like a new cheap version of the *Bunte* for half-educated big-headed hordes of critical nurses and no longer completely daisy-fresh enlightened pedagogues under the Porsche-speed-demon leadership of Ulf Poschardt, intended to get the publisher's hooks deeper and more cynically and mendaciously into the senior citizen advertising demo than the old

Bunte had done and thus to pull it into the red, with a totally distinct approach from any new ultranationalist thing – his comparative study of the territorial, military, and Prussian facets of assorted skinheads has made this appear to him somehow undervalued. Just now the exact argument doesn't look so extremely exact, however it must be said at present that perhaps that's not so totally SUPER crazy important.

Let's talk instead about the frankly marvellous mood that prevails today when you sit in the most beautiful June weather in the afternoon in front of Monte Sol on the Spanish island of Ibiza and read today's papers solo and with a friend. The German newspapers. The effect is different here. It somehow hits the spot, you just have to recommend it to everyone.

Then, no less amused, we amused ourselves about the *drug baron*, as we called him then and there for the very first time, about the whole sinister drug-baron aura, which proceeded from the drug baron himself but above all from the term *drug baron*. We're now his prisoners, BTW.

Then we trashed the newspapers and bought a map of the island and drove the mopeds to Santa Gertrudis.

That's what the place is called.

In the agreed-upon café, which can't be missed: first polish the sunglasses, then put the sunglasses on. On the flight out, we bought *Men In Black* sunglasses in the duty free shop, just now on the island they give just the right optic, lax and laughable, ludicrous, downmarket and trashy-cool. With this kind of sunglasses in Munich you'd look like someone from journalism school or a Falkenberger or a *tz* editor.

Now this little Malay chick comes over to wait on us,

anyway that's what we think she looks like. The whole café is really nothing but this muggy open-air terrace where we, the lone guests, are sitting. All around us is bright bast, flashy flags, rubbish and bric-a-brac and all the things the heart desires, and the place is called *Berize* and apparently belongs to some dude from Dusseldorf. You can see it right there on the map. We look at the map, look up, study the location, and conclude in unison it might well be most enjoyable if not actually the most enjoyable thing of all if we were to start off by getting just a little tiny bit loose. So we get them to bring us a Campari Orange, in accordance with the law of the land. Everything always strictly in accordance – by now there's no longer any debate about that, right – with the law of the land.

The warm buzz you feel by the third sip belongs, as is generally known, in second place just behind the constant, unbroken buzz, as a kind of buzz especially well cultivated among holiday-goers on holiday. You don't have to do anything, just keep drinking them down nice and easy, at the key moment, of course.

Hm. Tasty.

'Two more Campari-and-orange, please.'

'Excuse me, we're waiting here for a Mr Kara Ben Neemsie or Nimmsie. Any chance he's already been by?'

The Malay laughs, doesn't understand us.

We have the boss come over.

Oops.

This old queen walks up, talks our ears off. On his T-shirt you see the words: *Feuer und Flammen für diesen Staat*. He's got a Bavarian-style alienated prince-regent's or Führer's birthday beard on his face, over the T-shirt he's wearing a short-sleeved Hess-celebration hoody.

Fatter than Elvis, with a voice like Michael Jackson. More than a few screws loose. Simply superb.

He informs us: Yeah, that guy, right, yeah, he'd been there before, had asked after two guys from Munich, didn't introduce himself, didn't leave a message either. And then he drove off in the direction – Oh! Really! In THE direction?! – in this like pinkish white ginormous American convertible-type thing. He didn't really know anything else about it, unfortunately. He couldn't tell us anything else. No.

'That's just wonderful, Mr – '

'Strelitz,' he said.

'Right. Thanks a lot. And please bring us another four of them Campari-and-oranges. And the bill. We've got to get going right after.'

'I'll have it right over.'

'Much obliged. Thanks.'

The White Album was playing in the background, by The Orb, the other side, the so-called bright side of the moon. Conversation about music: what quantity of kitsch best serves to improve the mood? When does it turn cloying, sticky, obtrusive?

Olaf suffers, like most of the better DJs, from an ultra-refined fine-chiselled finical feel for musical elements. Its judgements turn ever more differentiated, ever more nervous, and ever truer – but may finally collapse into this collapsing of the truth where you wind up automatically with some monstrous marriage of vapidity and classicism, Goethe and Detroit, Chicago and the ancient Greeks. That doesn't add anything, doesn't go anywhere. It has nothing to do with the now.

It's summer, and every afternoon I go to Olaf's record shop, the Boy, and the first thing I say is: Olaf, bring out the hits. And Olaf turns giddy and plays the weirdest super-early or super-late house records that only just came out somewhere and you can get hold of them at so-and-so's place via some madly complicated import-export chicanery, and there are only or might only be – at most, I swear – one and a half units in all of Germany or Southern Swabia or whatever, and so on.

No complaints there.

Everyone meets HIS record dealer somewhere, the one who takes you back into history and at the same time gives you a thorough education in taste-formation and music. Thanks, Uncle Olaf. Then comes the argument, always around the question: What are you supposed to do now with everything, with this knowledge, with these refined appraisals, with these many highly specialized developments and investigations? What is the goal supposed to be? Not classicism, anyway, not research, not final truth. Minimal reductions of some reducibility or other.

The goal should be – platitude or not, who cares – a full-throttle-programme that examines all coarseness and crass banal effects on a single plane, as the highest and most outlandish specialist-specializations do. That's the hard thing, though, and when it comes off, it's actually always the craziest one, too: to strive for, at least to search for, to permit to occur, to create, to find, this single plane for what are essentially mutually exclusive aesthetic programmes and effects. Please, though: at least try for the right thing.

Because you can't just say to everyone: I'm this kind of freak, I make this kind of necklace, sometimes I sell three or four during the day out on the beach. That is shit, that's the last straw.

This freak though – change of scene, back to the beach – passes us a lump of hash as he laughs there among his hand-painted multi-coloured necklaces, so we do the deal fast, pay and make off with the chunk. The freak's speaking Swiss dialect and he laughs again and stands up out of his Indian squat and walks on up the beach and squats back down by the next group and offers his goods to them.

Did someone somewhere say something against this kind of freak?

We get some papers and roll and smoke. The Campari Soda buzz slowly dissipates. The music today seems more demanding than yesterday.

Melodyterror.

And too many human voices singing to boot. That ruins even the hottest track. The English malady: some-time or other some fat soul singer just has to shriek something and turn every track into a song. Even if it's the darkest drum and bass, like earlier, when we were listening to Tim Simenon or 808 State. Ground rule: the woman's voice comes in and the musicality crashes, goes bye-bye, never to be seen again.

I walk to the beach bar to buy an ice cream, and the guy at the bar says something in Spanish, about the drug baron, obviously.

'Olaf, come over here, I can't understand this dude.'

Olaf comes over, he doesn't understand Spanish either, but at least he can speak it a little. Turns out we're either supposed to wait here, like yesterday, or go. Which one wasn't clear.

Super-info.

You got my number.

Claro. I'll keep my mobile on.

Stellar, dude.

Good thing we had just talked about that right before. For reals.

The DJ horde grows bigger and bigger, we lie there in the midst of it while the rest of the beach people pack it in and leave. Night's falling in Salinas.

Olaf is talking with Jens Lissat, talking about Königsburg, which is HIS Königsburg, where everything just flows for him, where he gets everything. And he does his thing there, that is truly cool. He introduces us to a cute chick, his girlfriend. And he and Martina get along like totally super. Lying next to me is a so-called DJ Jauche from Berlin. Everything in Ibiza is way too commercial for him.

DJs from all of Germany flock together here, because *Ibi!* – as people from Munich say tenderly, perhaps Anki's the one who coined that – has become, over the last few years a kind of reception-and-party camp for techno-orphans of all stripes and all classes. Especially people from the west and south are here. The northerners find Ibiza too slummy, they'd rather just fly straight to Miami. And for the easterners it's not or is no longer pristine, the spirit's gone, or it's just not underground enough.

On to the right, towards the back, over towards the dunes, the English DJs are gathered; and the giant gang of English ravers, the hardest-nosed party comrades, have set up shop there, too, and it's all drugs, shagging, fighting, and sunburn, to quote Irvine Welsh. The local island DJs and the Spanish and Italians are in the middle of all that.

And everywhere and for everyone: the spirit of the obligatory DJ conversation, the customary, ritualistic, formalized, classic drawn-out DJ conversation, repeatedly repeated with relish. How cool it was at the last DJ party at such-and-such a place, the location alone was legend, and the people, and the way the people flipped out at the very point in time when the person talking had taken over; like before that, it was basically just sort of blah, to be honest, the DJ before, I mean, right, you don't want to just slag off your colleagues, anyway maybe just a little bit before then he'd seen and interpreted the whole vibe differently, doesn't matter; anyway, after a few tracks – especially the magic record, you know the one you hadn't even thought of at first, that you'd previously looked at in a whole different context, but that all at once revealed itself differently, a totally unexpected stroke of luck – the person talking had just grabbed the helm firmly and steered the party out of choppy waters and set the ship aright again; and so it was like actually there was like celebration and shouting once again, no-one had actually seen it that way for a long time, maybe, to be really honest never. But anyway the new record the person talking had chosen had been a high point, no doubt, that one was coming up next, the guy had played it into a DAT recorder he had brought himself, just to hook that up had been an adventure-odyssey on its own, to be honest a totally singular and self-contained multi-volume roman-fleuve, basically; plus the dubplate from DJ So-and-so, who is sitting just two ears away, halfway eavesdropping, anyway he dug it, one hundred per cent, super brutal, really the best thing, this is just my opinion now, would have been to check the people's reaction to that evening, I mean like I said, we're talking this legendary public from such-and-such and so on and so forth.

Another aria was about the fees. The offer that was an insult in itself, one you'd just have to deal with again, how many Ks you'd been paid here and there, for an hour and a half somewhere in the pampa, in this hillbilly disco, and how even then the stuff you did was actually like really fresh, you did right by these weird moustachioed hillbilly organizers. Excursus on the decline of the scene, the fault of these hillbilly disco lowlifes.

Plus, an expansive *lamento* about the general plummeting of fees all over these last two years. Even this dude and that dude had to go small-time now.

And the other organizer, Tom says to Eric, had also had dealings with so-and-so the booker, and with the success of her label's last performance she was flying high, and that was especially stupid and hard to swallow. And it turns out this particular booker was trying to rip everyone off the same way over the phone, and that was working wonders for the underground cred of the label whose underground DJs and acts she was hawking.

She obviously feels totally professional and savvy doing this. And it never even occurs to her that every individual she's called on the phone, each of whom she's tried to swindle individually, will in five minutes have retold her entire swindling text to five-times-five different individuals, and so she tries to retract her lies under the scrutiny and profoundly disparaging appraisal of some five-to-the-fifth people from the nearby vicinity, half of whom she will have back on the phone in the days to come, without realizing what all of them have all learned in the interim etc.

To Wolli: the bottom line is, in the long run, especially in the business world, we've seen this in the nightlife, which as far as professional careers go may actually boast the most highly concentrated assortment of bums, failures, dropouts, losers, and desperados you can find – the bottom line is, there are no dirty tricks. They always end up flopping. In the long term, they just don't cut it.

But at first you always think things are different, over and over you say: Lying and cheating, trickery, rip-offs, fucking the other guy over – that's what the business world boils down to. But it doesn't. And getting the partners and the competition all heated and maliciously turning them against each other, all these cool or supposedly cool tricks, are NOT the higher mathematics of cynically scheming moneymaking business standards. They're just bullshit, kid's stuff. And unsuccessful to boot.

The higher mathematics is something totally different, something completely simple: knowing that every cent, real or imagined, that passes through your real or imaginary company's hands is the carrier of highly explosive information, that the entire SPIRIT of the company hangs on and will never cease to hang on every cent received or paid or even just negotiated and calculated, and will circulate far and wide, wherever you make things happen with your money. With this as a basis, calculations of self-interest yield an optimal, totally real, and unidealistic morality. Everyone knows everyone knows everything about everyone, as far as business goes, of course, and consequently everyone behaves, in concrete terms, reasonably, without malice, realistically.

The one precondition: you must actually be fascinated with money, with its strange, secretive nature, you must also be drawn of course to the music of the balance sheet, and above all, and much more so, you must take a very basic joy in the study of the movement-structure of money, which externalizes the monetary interiority preserved in money itself into the world in monetary terms.

Many people with utterly different ideals and interests, be they political, scientific, artistic, take no interest in money in this sense: totally clear. But it's weird, ridiculous, and in effect a total joke when these people with their uptight contempt for money try to engage in monetary and social undertakings in their peculiarly and perfectly tricky, arrogant, and asocial way. But no-one lets the contradiction between political ideals and malice in human-social terms bother them. That is what's so strange, politically, about all of this.

Question, even if this story has already been told to death: Name a writer who has written for the cool politics rag *Konkret* who hasn't been stalled, put off, and lied to forever and three days by *Konkret* and its preposterous boss – the transfer went out yesterday, I have the carbon copy right here in front of me – and on and on goes the stalling until you finally either forget or it quite simply becomes too miserable to have to go on with ten threatening, inquiring, degrading phone conversations.

Then again, anyone who knows anyone who's ever written for the *Spiegel* can ask them how that works; how with no stupid dawdling or runarounds they pay a proper honorary on the spot when the piece comes out, and if not then a no less realistic kill fee. What a wonderful mood such relationships bring. How reasonable and normal this seems. And the simple reason for this, plainly said, is that Augstein, although he would gladly be a cynic, has become, probably thanks to the pressure possession of money brings, an upstanding person.

That's what I tell Wolli. My informant in no-mercy-before-the-enemy matters. Take off, full throttle, no dil-ly-dallying, try everything, come what may, who the fuck cares. Where do we go then to look for the next mistake we can try our hand at next time?

Our courier has been located and has handed off the in-famous bag, a little red gym bag with *Ibiza Island* printed on it in white.

Aha.

Then he beats a retreat. And there were a couple of books and cassettes and threads inside. For this guy and that. In Frankfurt. And was he correctly informed of the agreement with Marc that we would take it with us when we flew out tomorrow.

'Yes.'

Everything in English, just a little bit broken.

The guy is no Spaniard, he looks like Snoop Doggy Dog, but not black, totally white, actually, with pale skin and this sharp-sly-horny thing going on, sorry. Olaf leads the negotiations, negotiates with the guy, they smoke. Modalities: this, that, the dude in Frankfurt, the handoff, us, pay in, pay out, so on and so forth. NOT pleasant.

'Yes, yes.'

'NO!'

'OK.'

I say tell Olaf something in German. The courier looks at us sceptical and laughs. Maybe we'd be better off leaving the bag with the guy here, actually, then he can just take it to Frankfurt himself. Olaf nods gracious-ly, he's got other plans.

While they're talking, Spoon rolls in and goes up to the chick sitting next to me. Her name's Stefanie Giovinetti, she's from Hamburg and is in year ten at the so-called Heinrich Hertz School, or that's what she told us earlier anyway in her polished debutante-Hamburgese.

Spoon sits down next to her and is totally charming with her, and the chick's face lights up faintly in response. And Spoon tells her about the full moon party today at one of the beach bars over past this one place, not too far from here. Everyone was going to be playing there, him, Sven, Goodgroove, Pauli, and there was a whole gang of people from Frankfurt on the island, and he had been thinking, since he'd seen her and all, they'd all really like it if she'd come to this party too. Well said, right? So what does she think?

Yeah. Uh. Mm.

She doesn't know, her parents, her friends –

Spoon is already talking: Done deal, she's in. And he says something about punch and the moon, about bright lights, about the mood and all, and especially about how cool everything will be tonight. Then he gives her a romantic look.

All this naturally in meticulous Hessian. A language that was indubitably the reigning raver Esperanto for one or two years throughout the Bundesrepublik wherever rave conversations were held. We're talking, I'd wager, from '91 to '92, something like that.

Anyway, Spoon now has a light-blue Xeroxed flyer in his hand with a printed description of the place for the girl. She says she'll take a look, and Spoon eyes her up and kisses her on the mouth real quick and stands back up with a cheerful heart. And the chick studies the flyer.

Before Spoon goes, he gives us this same flyer and says people should meet at the Dome for it, but earlier rather than later. Some of the Frankfurt guys would be heading out from there in their cars. Probably most likely maybe even definitely there'd be room for someone or other.

'Especially for you,' he says to the chick and goes. And she laughs again and asks whether I know the Dome. And where it is. And what's up with it and so on.

Meanwhile, it's finally night. An old track by Hypnotist is coming out of the bar, the one with the rainbow that's like:

let it flow
let it go
because I know
that's the only way
I know
that you can see rainbows –

And it seems to me as if the music has just turned louder somehow, and the people are fewer and fewer, and the light grows more and more intense. And then all the colours glow again here all high-colourful and totally strong.

And the sea comes slowly closer.

Later we're sitting at the Dome, or in front of it, on the black terrace, and it's just after twelve. The drug baron is explaining how tonight all hell has broken loose all over town because of the Full Moon.

The Full Moon is an invention of the local seventies disco, Pasha. They actually hand out their own Full Moon Calendar. Notably useful if you have some kind of pus in some kind of cavity, they say pus is influenced by the moon, just like blood. There are apparently women who feel somehow affected by these things with the moon, sexo-technically speaking. A normal person can hardly imagine it.

The drug baron runs down an exhaustive list of all

the parties taking place today, then which parties he would hit up, in which order, and why, and which not and why not.

And above all how it is WAY too early for right now for this place, for the Dome. Being here before two o'clock was a straight-up mistake.

Aha. Sure. Whatever he says.

Tourists, twinks, trannies, and flat beer: that's what you get for like 14 marks. A clear-cut case: best thing is you go ahead and get drunk, a little bit, just a little bit at least, to pre-orient yourself, to ease yourself in. Then this slight pressure in your head goes away, and the cigarette trembles way less when you're smoking it and it's being smoked.

Here's the beer. 'Cheers.'

And along comes Stefanie from before, from the beach, and now she's got two friends with her and a dude who keeps calling her 'Steffi.' Sounds super sweet.

'Hey, Steffi!'

Steffi introduces the others, and we introduce ourselves, and suddenly I see what I had seen before, but not so clearly marked out: that these here are classic specimens of the venerable Hamburg preppy-milieu, a style which, like all pregnant styles, has long since eternalized into an eternal style that even exists now, with minor deviations, in Dusseldorf and of course also in Munich. You can't really hate a thing like that, though. That plump little thing with her bits of leftover baby fat.

Lambswool pullover, could be cashmere too, of course, dark blue or beige, white men's shirt, super-simple pearl necklace, brand-name jeans, black or dark-red penny loafers, no heels, obviously. Not even the unavoidable 'P' word is missing, nor the so heavily hyped

'L' word. More silence, babe, less talk. That says more than a thousand words.

Naturally the parents are divorced, doesn't matter though, Daddy pays, worships his little daughter, foots the bill for everything, thanks Poppy, one of each please, thanks again. And after six months on the scene, what am I saying, after three, they go from zero to a hundred, turn into the hardest, hardest-boiled fucked uppest party vamps, with the hardest drug-decline and the most laid-back man-eater vibe.

Right. So then two years pass, and they've got their photos in 'Talk of the Town' in *Prinz*, and they make it into *Die Zeit* once and then here comes the *Stern* with its series: *Germany's Youth Scene, Chapter 74*, and they get their picture taken for it, get interviewed by some hack or other, get used in the crummiest way possible for the same old *Stern* fabrications and the same old *Stern* lies, but naturally they couldn't give less of a fuck, there they are, and for a brief moment they are like actually famous, not even nineteen yet and they've really actually seen it all and had it all already, they've done it all and taken it all, understood it all and witnessed it all and re-told it a hundred thousand and one times. It happened. And that suffices.

Then they're over it, they're bored with it. The night-life as a whole, the repetitiousness, the bores. The shitty drugs, the eternal hangover, and the same old hollow text texted up everywhere by everyone. The same stupid film that's running nonstop. It's boring. It's just like, boring, everything.

And so they go back to school, which they dropped out of from an excess of exuberance, and soon they've even done their college entrance exams. So they can study, of course, and study they do. Biology. Or behavioural science. Or film, but if it's film, it's gotta be San Francisco.

Marry rich, live good, have pretty kids.

And after five minutes, the kids are fourteen, and they start going out in turn.

Lovely.

Just nice.

'Hey, Steffi, you sweet little cute little bear cub, won't you finally introduce us to your lovely little friends.'

Spoon talking. The Frankfurt crew is here. We take off.

Olaf and I are sitting in a rented van in the second row of seats in the back, the others are driving off somewhere else, and there's extra wild music roaring, super hard Neo-Hard-Trance, then the most brutal Gabba Funk. The vehicle belongs to some dudes from Gelsenkirchen who have a record distributor there attached to a magazine or something. And I try to ask Olaf about the four thousand marks the drug baron insisted on forcing on us before. Now we've got the money and we've got this ridiculous bag around our necks. Which literally means: it's in the hotel. That's no good at all. That is quite simply ridiculous.

The driver keeps turning and bellowing something. And the people on the seat in front of us bellow back to him. It seems we've suddenly got lost. A gas station pops up out of the night, inconceivably, and everyone gets out in the middle of the night and buys beer and cola. The trip goes on. The beer cans hiss and we look at the pills the Doggystyle dude gave us before. Conceived as a confidence-building exercise, presumably.

Half a pill? A whole pill? What time is it?

And then a bit of dithering, not much, fuck it, it's

already just after one: Everyone take a whole one, al-
leyoop. Cheers. Hopefully they find the party now,
otherwise it's looking grim, on account of the music
alone.

And so we're sitting there in the back in the furthest
back seat and looking up at the road, at the stretch of it
the headlights light up and make quiver. Curves, hills,
woods, bushes. And no land in sight, no beach bar, no
party, and the drive drags on and on. And the crazy tape
playing continuously, and the roars of our friends from
Gelsenkirchen. We look at each other now and then and
take a swig.

Oh yeah.
   Wow –... – hmm... – you –
   whatchamacallit –
   yeah –
   me too –...

Hours later: the memory of the scent of the sand near
the sea. The car park. The distant, thick-gracious bass-
boom-beat, which says: Now we've finally got it. And at
this moment with every new beat and heartbeat, with
every breath drawn into the lungs, with every breath-yes
and breath-no, with every pulse and palpitation of the
eyelids and with every next step and the one following,
exploding all at once like in high-speed slo-mo, the pill
took hold with stunning force. Alone, the path that follows the car park towards the beach bar appeared to me
like a great sumptuous sensational sojourn, which could
calmly last a few hours or days, for all I cared, so pleasant the night-time air was here now, the bright-sparkling
sky and the seduction of anticipation. And it endured
in that same moment and drew on and I didn't want to

146

hang back, instead I thought: Keep going, how beautiful, and I did keep going. With every step, with every boom, every boom boom boom, I felt the wings that wing us onward when we walk. The feeling of comfort around us, the pine flooring that was there, the party coming nearer to us. And here, before us, already now passed by: new fresh time.

Short exchange of glances with Olaf: No words, or...?
Absolutely. The Hammer.
Simply cool.

Later I saw this scene, a woman was dancing back and forth on the wooden tree branch holding up the pergola over the dance floor. She was like rocking back and forth on the beam. And I couldn't grasp this image: tree, Eve, apple, serpent. Temptation. Knowledge.

What's all that supposed to mean?
Tree?
With the feeling that what's being announced is something cool for everyone.
That it will yet be revealed, even to me.

MAY YOUR BODY COME

The girls are lying there, as described, and wave. They are lying under a very specific, gigantic tall beech with broad branches in the English Garden on the outer edge of the baseball field with a view of the monopteros, but not right in front of it.

Girls. What that means here is: three very grown up, slightly worn out, thoroughly seasoned from long years of service to the night life, at this point slightly sexually-salaciously vitalized by anything and everything, no longer especially young young women just hanging out on their own.

Pretty, knowing, and a little bit desperate.

Who wouldn't be? In our place?

Rick thinks, then waves back. And walks up to them across the meadow.

Sunday afternoon.

English Garden. Munich.

Around two o'clock.

Same time, different place: Pulverturm.

The Pulverturm.

The Pulverturm lawn, behind the Pulverturm, the lawn behind the car park behind the Pulverturm, THE lawn.

Medium-high grass. Groups. And chicks from around here. And things yet unknown. Different things in different combinations that are still new.

The enchanted garden.

World of flowers, bees, and kittens.

Aromas.

I act out a little sex dramolette with Nicole.

She is my older sister.

We boil tea for the kid in the kitchen.

We warm up water for a hot water bottle.

She stands, I sit.

Like Hansel and Gretel, we walk out to the forest, into the underbrush to look for berries, to the brook, where it smells.

Later it struck me I had completely forgotten to even consider asking myself what SHE thinks, how she sees herself.

Her playing, continuous.

Nicole shows me her mother's esoterica books. A whole shelf full of tarot and so on.

We are sitting in Jenny's teensy-weensy Fiat, like six of us, driving from the hotel to Popkomm.

It's hot, yeah, again, with jerking and stuttering as we drive.

Kathrin is on my lap, we're sitting up front, and we're spraying some kind of weird local anaesthetic into each other's mouths, far back in the back, then taking deep breaths. It gives you this crazy kind of flash, but it also hurts like hell.

We hadn't listened to any music the whole night long in the hotel, so the tape is like an authentic spiritual liberation, something brilliantly soft and soothing, tenderly enveloping, too long missed, protecting and consoling, as if music were truly an existential human need.

And the sun burns on the car roof, in the gridlock, in the traffic in the city. And this burden on me, on my leg and belly, a pleasant weight. I just need to shift my leg.

'Would you please spray some more of that crazy shit in my mouth?'

Back in the hotel we'd been running around in front of each other, naked because it was so hot, and we'd also been in the bathtub together.

We were sweating from the heat, from the inexorable heat, from the nocturnal heat of early midsummer nights when no-one could help but sweat.

Then, all superhot, we had to take a bath in a hot bathtub: nice.

Kathrin talks about how she perceives her life, what all her plans are, her ideals and her dreams. How there's something weird about her spinal column. She shows it to us then, Sigi is also up, she shows her breasts, too. Tells us what she thinks about them. Her breast-thoughts, if you will.

Everything about Kathrin looks dope, fulfilled, stunning. She radiates all this when she talks with her entire body. Bill's sleeping, someone's laid out next to Bill. And the three of us are sitting practically naked on the second bed of a frankly quite small double room in the Braunschweiger Hof hotel in Cologne and talking super soft, super gentle, about everything.

Secretive brotherly-sisterly mood.

Understanding: Sweet.

The *woman*. Unbelievable. I hadn't really totally got that before now.

The woman-thing. What a totally cool thing it is.

It was something new to me.

I knew nothing about it.

Straight-up bewildered we wander aimlessly around Popkomm, through the halls and hallways. I've forgotten where I was supposed to go, where I meant to go. Where I am.

I look around.

I've lost my orientation.

I don't know anything anymore: where, how, what, why, where to.

Feelings of vertigo, tumbling.

Suddenly an idea comes to me as a salvation: just sit down briefly on the floor and flip out.

Exactly.

That was it.

Comfy, and I'll get warmed back up.

In the distance now I see a group of Spexers coming. Aha, sure sure. Break out in sweat. I wonder whether

I should stand up. Wipe the sweat from my forehead. My forehead is ice-cold. I feel too drained to meet the Spexers on my feet.

Here they are.

Friendly laughter descending on me from above, saying something, asking.

I prevaricate. 'What now?'

I have the feeling I'm not really getting what they're saying. And for me that is somehow degrading and torturous.

I ask myself: Do they really not even realize how nice it would now be if they would leave me alone right now at this instant?

Ask myself: How long has this scene gone on already?

Might my sense of time be totally off-kilter?

When Diedrich comes over, I pull myself together and stand up. Stand teetering and tottering in front of Diedrich, and he chatters on to me like nothing's up at all.

I make an effort at interpretation: He thinks it's politest just to politely overlook my plainly pretty deranged state and go on like nothing is up.

Discard this interpretation.

He's talking like he always does.

I notice: he hasn't even noticed anything.

He's talking.

Brutal torture, fucked up scene.

Diedrich is talking about a new *Spex* lexicon they've been working on that they're presenting here at Popkomm.

Oh?

Yeah.

Cool.

Like the foreign minister of a quite distant allied country I share with Diedrich in due form that all of that is and must be totally wonderful and super-interesting to boot but the thing is unfortunately it happens that just now I have to sit down on this very spot, on the floor here or actually anywhere for all I care.

Friendly bewilderment from the friend I am friends with.

Recoil, pause, an 'eh'.

Then I manage to grab his shoulder and say: 'Diedrich, as you can see, I'm not doing so hot.'

And I laugh, and he laughs, I think, now, too.

We say a brief goodbye to each other.

And then I turn quite slowly around, and think again: Dammit, where the hell am I? And walk off, doesn't matter where. As purposefully as I can. And attempt while walking continually to gather some data, to orient, to integrate and assimilate it, with the idea of perhaps figuring out how I can get back OUT of here as quickly as possible.

At the moment, that would be the best thing, I think.

To get out of Popkomm as quick as I can.

Ah, an usher.

I see an usher.

And just as I am steering towards the usher with absolute concentration, Jutta pops up before me. In this like cowboy shirt. She stands there just in front of me and bugs out her eyes, Jutta eyes, and all around them her long Jutta hair. And she shouts: 'Rainald!', spreads her arms, facepalm, laughs, and says, 'Look at you! What's going on with you?'

And I think: Finally. Thank you. Yes.

The first normal person I've run into here.

And she looks at me and asks in the most gracious and completely unaffectedly caring and serious way: 'Is everything OK with you, or...'

And I just nod, and am thankful, and speechlessly happy, and think: So THIS is what she's like, this woman, how cool. I had always looked at her totally different. Well – that was clueless. She's totally different.

Lovely.

And I go on wandering around.

So I finally grasp it. That there is something else beyond eternal boyish bravado. A – yes, really – a kind of delicacy, maybe only seven seconds long, a moment of gossamer fleeting intimacy proffered and given as a gift, just like that, as a simple generosity, a customary balsam for the partied-out flotsam of the night before.

This always occurs to me now whenever I think something nasty about Jutta.

Now everything goes by easy.

I walk to the usher, ask where the exit is, and listen to his response.

The usher gives his explanations and while doing so makes all sorts of hand gestures.

I say my thanks to the usher.

I give up the plan of leaving Popkomm. Because just now it honestly seems too stressful. But it doesn't have to be. I don't have anywhere to go. And I enjoy the inner calm coursing through me now in waves, and I float there through these indistinguishable halls, a fine thing, this.

I notice how once again everything just comes together and clicks.

And I even actually catch sight of – who can describe my delight, my joy, my coming into bloom – my beloved

Wolli strolling up to me quite calmly with his slack, splay-legged sailor's gait, joyous, his way.

'Dude! Wolli! Finally! Good to see you!'

'Where we headed?'

'To drink.'

'Def.'

And then we sit in the late afternoon sun somewhere outside and drink beer and toast each other.

NEVER LONELIER

a little foretaste, little doll –

than in August,

hour of plenitude in the

poem unspooling nimbly inside me.

This specific circumstance of a highly agitated kind of nervous concentration:

What has happened so far?

What have we done?

What are the consequences?

What has even occurred here so far?

And hearing overhead, in the tranquil air, your: Hh... hhh... haa haa....

It isn't

hard, talki...

Let alone to react, but not TOO edgy, not too fast.

On board with the plan.

But what exactly was that plan?

Change plans.

Let yourself go, hold back.

quick and mellow –

En bref: it's a shining, calmly scalding Sunday afternoon in June, and at the monopteros and at Pulverturm and in the toilets at Labor, in beds under sheets, and even in M.B.'s hotly heated attic apartment in the Hohenzollernstrasse, there, and in a thousand other places not so easily named, in all places at one time, all eyes upon it, wanders the ghost of happening, the magnet of longing, now here, now there.

Sings its song like. I can –
I can move
move any mountain.

And in the Ungererbad, where the meadow stops, in the bushes, hears these voices whispering from the darkness of the leaves.

'I'm not up for it.'
'Why?'
'I don't know.'
'Pussy.'
Silence.
And whispered: 'Come on.'
They don't stir. They laugh.

The young woman in the hotel with the long straight hair, her head hanging upside down over the foot of the bed, and the way she stares with big eyes.

She waits, breathes, waits.

In Paris, along for the ride.

In a furnished room in Prague.

Up on the bunk bed, in a shared flat in Hamburg, in an old slightly ramshackle corner building by the fish market.

Bettine – Rheims – World – Feeling.

These patterns, this kind of colour, this sensation of space.

But: too much.

And: other bodies. Not so madly self-consciously intermingled in the everyday. Not so madly delicate and dubious.

Crazier. More normal.

More authentic.

And: WITH words. There's talk talk talk, but always about something else. Sister among sisters.

The young woman with the curly hair, the blonde in the bright little apartment, windows open, balcony door open, on the phone, standing there. She talks, hangs up. Lays the phone on the floor, undresses, and gets in the shower.

Ring.

She pushes the buzzer and stands there by the door. White boys' T-shirt, old gym trousers, dark blue, with holes. The bell rings. She hears the lift. It starts up, goes down, stops, goes back up, four floors. Comes to a halt.

She opens the door to the flat.

The dude comes up to her laughing. And she laughs back. They share a quick hug.

They sit in the kitchen and chat. He drinks water, she drinks beer. She sits on his lap, facing forward. She has a book in her hand and reads something aloud.

They go to the other room and lie down on the brightly carpeted floor next to the mattress and kiss.

It is a hot day.

Sometimes a gust of wind blows through the curtains hung in front of the balcony door and down onto the floor. Sucks in, blows out, dissipates.

They have undressed and are now lying next to each other naked.

They lie there enveloped, entangled.

Bodies, beautiful.

The bodies' action initiates and manipulates them automatically, lightly, very fast faster and faster.

Clear.

To the point.

Sensing the point of the other.

Somehow sex transforms into the joy of the intensification of pleasure, he becomes her, and she becomes him, as he can see through her. It feels like love.

Wet skin.

On your face, on your face.

On your belly and on your other belly.

In your hair and in your other hair.

Everyday talking and not talking and thinking of something else, and being somewhere else in thought, somewhere far, far away. Lying so gladly, so near the other now.

Snoozing together, middle of the day.

Sleeping together.

Two who don't know each other.

She is the one with the dark, closely cropped hair, the bright-orange overalls, the white bodysuit underneath, the Russ Meyer monster shapes. And she is sitting on top of him, big and heavy, ponderous, and unbuttons the front of her so-called bodysuit now, down the middle, and slides it up and out the sides.

She talks.

He says: 'But I'm – you know.'

She gets on top of him.

He concentrates.

The monster shapes, the child's perspective. The mad act of the older people earlier.

She talks to him. He'd also –

Something or other –

He should play along, right now.

OK.

If you say so.

Happy to get an order like that, get told where to go, how. Directness, no games, awesome. The coolest women of all: the ones who just pounce on those they have chosen whenever they think it's right to.

But unfortunately: at that moment he sees in the unbuttoned bodysuit pulled out in front of him an image of misery; in the flesh beneath, the epitome of all conceivable futility or if not, at least a lot of it.

The bald dark giant buttons on the front of her bodysuit back up quite amicably and business-like. Strange gymnastics on top of him, very close.

And the scent.

At the pond, the Faulen See.

'You don't love me.'

'I disgust you.'

'Don't you want to grab me?'

'You don't think I'm pretty anymore.'

'You just don't love me.'

You talk too much.

The pageboy chick and the one dude, and the two from the Babalu toilets, now at Fortuna, with other others, each in their respective masses. Her and her and him and him, and him and her and her and him etc. etc., everyone lying there in the dark at the far end of the room, dozing, in the niches with the sofas.

The classic after-hours sound is playing loud and pleasant, with hits and thuds and waves, monotonous, ONE sound, immutable, the entire time, for hours on end.

And they are lying there, all of them all tangled up together, knotted over and under each other, and each and every one of them is touching each and every other one somewhere, softly, normal, really.

But it's not completely normal. There's affection there.

We are in the kingdom of the kingdoms from before: in the early kingdom of the entire sense of movement, in the kingdom of the senses. And everywhere there are two hands in movement together, and other parts, arms, legs, armpits, and other recesses that lie together and rub against each other and sometimes rub together harder, and two not yet completely familiar bodies approach and feel each other out. They unite, they wander together from place to place.

One lays a hand on the other on that little belly of hers, there, and proceeding southwards from the navel, rises over a soft convexity and soon sinks back down close to the cusp of the pelvic bone, so teensy weensy and superfine.

The way that feels for both of them.

Not moving. Now moving.

Now, super-soft.

They move so softly that the interpretive possibilities remain open, just as if they hadn't moved. This gives them both freedom.

The fingertips sometimes graze the upper edge of the thicket of hair. When they do, a kind of inner giggling occurs in the body parts, perhaps through the possibility of stimulation thus suggested, the stimulation itself. You could then quickly do something hard, brutal, ironic, to sidestep the categorical instance in which some follow-up would follow.

Naturally everything could stop immediately or start over again once more from the beginning.

The game is in essence a game of games.

It is played in a world worked out prior to the priors.

It started on this hot Sunday afternoon on the meadow behind the Pulverturm, where I – I don't know how, how it happened, how exactly it actually occurred – met the girls. The girls: there were three of them. You didn't necessarily remember their names.

Probably we had all taken drugs somewhere the night before, maybe though we had also come straight from home, fresh from the bathtub, all showered and cold, showered and lotioned up. It was the summer after the raid, when the Pulverturm thing was just starting to really take off. Just like that one summer when all summer long you could meet everyone at the Chinese Tower, that was the way this summer the Pulverturm issued its irresistible call and everyone followed along.

You hear something?

What?

The Pulvi's calling.

Yeah, I hear it too.

Come on, let's drive over to the Pulvi right quick.

At that moment you didn't even really know what was dragging you to the Pulverturm of all places or why. There were actually so many reasons not to go to the Pulverturm. But you just had this clear sense over and over of the allure of a beginning, the beginning of something that had not yet totally been clearly agreed on, the moment that lay BEFORE the moment of definitive import and comprehensibility.

What for?

No idea.

Cool.

And you were not yet so contrary or rather uncontrary enough just to follow, without all too many of the strange thoughts spawned while alone together with so many others, the secretive shifting peregrinations of the collective of companions of the night, to follow, just to follow, for the most part.

And then it happened on this Sunday night that we were sitting in the Pulverturm meadow, a little new gang of four to seven people who flocked and came and went around the girls in shifts, and I just stayed sitting there the entire afternoon, so ultra-pleasant was the mood.

I discovered a new thing: smoking up.

There's far too little smoking on this planet. That's what every smoker tells you. And I say to you: You just cannot get started early enough. People always forget how important it is to smoke, especially to start smoking at the right time. People always forget to take speed with it. And that makes smoking work way better.

All this was as yet unknown to me.

If you're a dude, it's girls who instil drug culture in you. The girls show you how it's done. That is, if you will, part of the so-called secret wisdom of women, which they practically pass down to us in practice. And sometimes, when you're into it, it works, and you just go along with it, you repeat what they showed you how to do, the beauties.

Like now and again, for example, how to roll one up at ease. And also, now and again, to do a little line of speed.

There are times when people's not entirely unfounded fear of the different nasal drugs disinclines them to say the word 'snort'. People prefer to say 'do' even if what you're doing is 'snorting'.

'You want to do a bit of speed, too?'

'Ooh, yeah, fantastic idea.'

The speed is lying on a cigarette box that is lying on a blanket that the girls are lying down over. And I bend down with the rolled-up ten note and concentrate on sucking in at the right moment.

Works splendid.

Just now, in the immediate aftermath, no immediate reaction follows ingestion, not a single thing that can be seen from outside. That's actually something every film nowadays gets wrong. Like most recently in *Clubbed to Death*, which we are talking about right now. The girls thought the love story a little bit forced. Obviously I liked the grunginess, the negativity. The fucked up scene, you know, the darkness, the dark vibe. I really found that so cool.

We talk about *Kids*.

We talk about *Trainspotting*.

Then about *Basquiat*.

Bienchen talks about *Below Zero*, which no-one else has seen.

We may affirm in general that the scope of the drugs and of the music world has not at all been portrayed exhaustively, satisfactorily, or even in broadly realistic terms in film. Now it hits Wolli that this could maybe be our calling, making this kind of film. And right away I say: What's the plot? Where are you going to come up with the plot for such a film, when in real life there actually is none?

Immediately everyone can think of a scene, then

162

another, then another right afterwards. Soon there's tons of them. Scenes and more scenes, a quantity of scenes comes together in no time.

And then our concentration turns slowly porous and finally abandons the theme. That's entertaining, it's so pleasant when you no longer have to concentrate because there's nothing for you to concentrate on.

I lay my head on Susi's upper thigh and breathe in the scent of grass.

Her majesty, the sun.

Together those the sun shines on become the summer, the great summer hum of many simultaneous years.

This is also the afternoon and maybe even the very hour when the young man in white, and naturally white leisure clothes, the young landed nobleman Gustaf Seibt, takes his weapon with the telescopic sight down from the curtain rod in his Berlin apartment in Kameruner Strasse, steps out onto the fourth-floor balcony, and from there aims at all the non-foreign and foreign children organizing their Sunday games en masse and shoots until all are dead.

Silence.

Later I'm sitting with Anki in the inner garden of the Pulverturm, we're leaning against the wall of the building and drinking wheat beer and talking about music and politics.

Concert of gazes. So say for example you see two people standing next to each other, both are looking in the same direction and each observes something there. Maybe a twosome has just seen a certain situation together and they exchange glances and now one is inquiring whether the other has noticed this situation, too, how this one young woman has followed with concern the look of the man standing next to her, because he has followed with interest the gestures of a very attractive and nearly naked young woman who has just made eye contact with him, or maybe someone behind him, while dancing; and as he turns around in vain to check on this potential partner, he falls within the supervisory gaze of the woman next to him, presumably his girlfriend, and now he is hastily shooting numerous swift glances at the faraway dancer girl to establish whether his girlfriend, who at this moment naturally is following his gaze, is capable of co-observing his original point of interest, because it is not entirely clear to him how long and how obvious his exchange of glances with the dancer girl has been, and the answer to the question of whether the dancer at this moment is still looking at him allows a certain conclusion to be sketched out, and then, when he actually still sees himself being looked at by the dancer girl, he hurriedly looks past her gaze somewhere further back, turns to his girlfriend, points to the back of the room and says something witty to her, and she, after taking a brief moment to tame her revulsion, beams at him cheerful-inquisitively, as if she hasn't even grasped everything she's just seen, and the two of them then hug warmly. And, as said, this one couple that has seen everything now checks with a brief and knowing exchange of glances whether they have caught the entire story from A to Z. And the first two, observing this exchange of glances, find themselves automatically drawn to the cute, nearly naked dancer girl, and without looking at each other an automatic smile crosses both their faces.

And so on and so forth etc. etc. –

Perversely fabricated as it sounds when it is retold, that is how ordinary and almost unconsciously normal it is, and this is something that is constantly occurring. Above all in places where many people are together without actually observing anything in particular, in a multitude in the midst of a mutually self-actuating exponentially potentiating mental energy, for each of these individual gaze-events touches on zillions of luminescent activities in the brain cells, emotions, thoughts, stories that reach back deep into the past, etc. etc.

which –

anyways –

fuck it, cheers, Anki –

Sorry for blabbing on to you so long.

It's just that I found all that so cool when I saw it at the last parade in Berlin.

So here's a quick brief discussion right quick about the observation we'd made about Love Parade that there was now practically no sufficiently overlooked position to allow one still to manage to do something secret. Something no-one sees. There was something nightmarish about that, but the very next moment you sense something calming in it. And when political and aesthetico-political journalism talks about the so-called 'masses', doesn't it really mean a way smaller gathering of people, a 'mob' or a 'horde' even? And when you really get a LOT of people together don't the civilizing and paralyzing forces grow so predominant that they generate an inability to act? A so-called 'mass' has probably never perpetrated even one single crime to date. The unending fascination with this concept of the 'mass', which is actually poorly suited to grasping a concentration or a gathering of people, naturally represents a fascination with fascism, and the fact is, there is something truly repulsive in this concept, in its political instrumentalization. The trajectory of this concept, its success, would be unthinkable were it not, despite its aura of critique, actually a blanket impression serving to excuse individual crimes and individual guilt. The immense reality of the simultaneous presence of a multitude of people, each in front of another, generates an immense IDEALITY even if only through the exponentially growing mental power of so many individual people through their gazes. Dangerous enough. But we always act as if it were the other way around: without action, an idea, a single idea, cannot murder, never. For all these reasons, if we are actually even meant to talk about the fact that VERY MANY PEOPLE are gathered together, the abstraction from this to the so-called 'mass', this concept purloined from the world of physics, is a thoroughly repugnant, hollow, and idiotic inanity. And we ask all the fine gentlemen who have recently uttered something indicating something or other along these lines, particularly in writing, to actually take a proper look at just such an assembly of very many persons, whether at the Pope's mass in Paris or at a Schürzenjäger concert in the Austrian Alps or at Love Parade in Berlin, and instead of lapsing right away into metaphorically governed observations, come up instead with real descriptions of what is actually there to be seen. Because just a fragment of the apprehension – which it is sadly hardly ever possible to realize fully – of all the soundless stories that emerge simultaneously among people in just a single second, even without their explicitly verbalizing them, is a fully authentic, vast REAL LIBRARY that leaves in the dust any fantasy library any fantasist could ever come up with, filled with practically all human motives, strivings, ways of encountering, and feelings, a hyper-detailed *corpus humanum*, an alphabet of all human and even inhuman human potential. And everyone who is actually present in such a place bodily and sees it with open eyes sees himself with revulsion and ecstasy amid this million-sharded mirror, is shaken and moved and inevitably must say something like: Yeah, that's me, I'm one of those, too. A so-called person.

How slowly you notice how the heat seeps in. From hot to heatsick to heat stroke.

Afternoon edges in, the air stands still. The still so immaculately mild early midsummer day turns quickly to an almost painful midmidsummer day, searing, paralyzed, paranoid.

And Rick has grabbed a six pack of beer from Café Mozart on the corner and is now heading to where Kim, Nadine, and Ayster are lying in the English Garden, and he sees them observe him and talk about him and laugh as they do so in the distance, and he doesn't really care, because now he notices how it feels while walking beneath the sun's heat as if he is hardly touching the so-called ground of the meadow in front of him, beneath him, and with each step, in slower and slower motion, he seems to be walking into some nightmare space, and for this very reason asks himself whether –

Ricky Martin. This is this young social scientist from the States, the one whose first big hit book, AGAINST EDUCATION – very successful in France as well, and what was then still called the DDR – caused a commotion on the American East Coast, with its sensitively pig-headed, intellectually rather dismal academic elite whose eternally rapt and envious gaze is fixed on the

Old World, like Susan Sontag before, perhaps, with her electrifying 1960's women's anthem, the much-ballyhooed MORE PENETRATION; then, a few years after AGAINST EDUCATION, he released a no less successful pederasty pastiche camouflaged as literature, LITTLE LETTERS TO ISABELLE, naturally people compared it right off with Nabokov, what's that book of his called again, whatever – wait, oh yeah, right: *Novel with Cocaine* – this Ricky Martin, who just now is working on his studies of intellectuals' fear of the body at the renowned Institute for Advanced Studies in Berlin, is sitting with *Spex* editor Tom Holert, Merz Academy professor Bazon Brock, and Albert Oehlen in the cafeteria at the Merz Academy in Stuttgart and drinking beer and talking.

With a presentation he has composed and certainly also thought up and is even personally presenting all on his own, Tom Holert is applying this afternoon for a so-called 'open position' as 'professor' at the Merz Academy before the assembled faculty and the directorship of the Merz Academy and, he feels, he has to say now, actually really quite good, all things considered.

'All things considered, it actually really went quite well, I must say,' he says.

This semester Professor Bazon Brock is back to organizing up-to-date PC weeks, today he's devoting himself in particular to the start of the new campaign under the motto: *This is a smoke-free building.*

A lovely thing.

Then and there, Ricky Martin lights one up, no apologies, he doesn't want the thing to go up in smoke. Kind students bring beer, bad music plays loud. When Rick speaks to Albert, Albert gives a quizzical look and says that he doesn't understand what Rick is saying, even though the two of them are sitting right next to each other. These are rather difficult circumstances for communicating.

The conversation, which had begun with the cinema and the deeply sensitive romantic drama called SEHERS OBSESSION and the grandiose, movingly histrionic delivery of the still quite young, enchanting, rightly celebrated German tragedian Urschi Altglas under the powerful spiritual leadership of Tom Holert, who had blossomed in this, their second film together, into a new, grander immediacy and broken passion, has taken a highly explosive turn into media criticism in general. In his particular subtle soft manner of speaking, Professor Holert introduces what is a, politically speaking, extremely radical PROFOUNDLY comprehensive completely independently formulated series of QUESTIONS probably NEVER yet formulated in this form even by himself, which, taken separately and as a whole, concern the fact that in certain articles on this year's Love Parade –

Rubbish.

Excuse me. Just kidding. Excuse me, Tom. What I mean to say is:

1. What is the point of media critique? Does it do anything? What? For whom?

2. Why not directly examine the things you're talking about?

3. Why, in so many putatively political analyses, does the fundamental fact of the observer's social position practically always escape consideration? Who they are and where they're speaking from, as an intellectual? What blind spots persist in the bits of wisdom they earn their bread by? This is old hat by now, the leftists

from the generation before us already grasped all that, all these insights.

4. Resolved: when you speak about the domain of the popular, particularly in regards to actually existing vulgarism and not only the abstracted pop distillate of whatever intellectual pop elite you belong to, then at some point, a collision is bound to occur: between your own intellectual form and the embodied reality of the vulgar. Thus there persists a mutual FEAR. And it is there, at this point between fear and threat, that REAL politics and reflection come together.

Naturally, as an intellectual, you can employ this fear for the sake of knowledge: as a distancing mechanism to help you more broadly dissociate your observations from the conclusions you derive from them. But this epistemological manoeuvre fails to resolve the basic problem: you are simply *a priori* INCOMPETENT and *per definitionem* INCAPABLE of recognizing, comprehending, and assessing many pop culture phenomena.

And all this may give you some sense of the intellectual profit to be had in examining the realia of the social world that is written about and talked about by individuals posing as pop culture writers and professors of so-called Cultural Studies and Communications with a wee bit less perspective and self-conscious critical *grandezza*.

5. Resolved: a minor addendum – nothing would be easier, writers always think, because they talk with other writers about other writers and the media in general, than firing off a bit of casual media critique. And then they inevitably get it wrong. Because in truth, it isn't all that easy to do well. Either you are super-pedantic, earnest, and dull, and you actually grapple with the thing argumentatively, or – more commonly

– in disagreement with the text to be critiqued, you address it in an ironic, citation-speckled tone, the tone of the pen-pusher who inevitably acts as though the work of argumentation was already taken care of ages ago and, as the pen-pusher's tone insinuates, you may simply forgo it, since everyone has long since reached an agreement about this, and on the basis of this basis which is no basis at all, you are free to babble on with winsome sogginess, at ease, until suddenly – yikes, it is here already? – the text reaches its end. That's that. And that is quite simply not enough. Instead of arguments, you offer grubby, very cheap, and hackneyed strands of general consensus from the figureheads of the dissenting collective of consensus dissenters. That's just a diversion for the bankrupt, intellectual pleasure for the poor in spirit. But, dear Tom, theirs is the kingdom of heaven, that's something, at least.

There the afternoon clouds gather now, splendidly bright, in plump forms.

A seed falls from the sky.

The grass is green, the trees are blue, the clouds yellow and grey and even red. Now is the hour when the gods, exhausted by the labours of the day, pair off in weary lust and vanish two by two. Then the bells toll in the Theatine Church, mad, heavy and wild and resonant, as if there were something here to be shared, something extremely urgent.

Poison lies over this world.

Beneath the copper beeches: the laughing women. They've shown Rick the thing with the so-called quarter. The ecstasy tab high you get from that is less psychedelic than light-hearted, warm, and above all more persistent.

For hours now, in the distance, the African drummers, camped out beneath a stand of trees in the other meadow, have suffused the hours with their beat, every second is a polyrhythmic tone sent forth laden into the breadth of the afternoon, multiplying the time for us.

Here too, it has been an endless afternoon, where exactly did it begin?

Yeah: Where? When?

Who cares?

DARK AND LONG, Underworld, the sound, the mood now.

Paperclip People: THE Summer.

STRANGE DAYS: the gaze, the new view of everything.

When I woke back up, I felt as though I had been reborn. I looked at the tree in front of me, looked at the clock, it was around three, and I didn't know whether I had slept half an hour or two hours. I stood up and was no longer woozy and I walked straight into the club. Anki came up to me, astonished:

'Where'd you get off to?'

'I had to go puke, I'm doing way better now.'

I went back out, bought a drink ticket, walked straight back to the bar, and ordered a cola. In the club now it was brutally hot and loud and the mood was cool. I walked through the impenetrably dark narrowly packed path with its boom and bustle up to the DJ booth. There was an American playing there, or an English or a French guy, I didn't know him. I walked over and asked someone:

'Who's that then?'

The sound was roaring and ruthless and just perfect for that moment, and of course I didn't understand the answer. I jumped off the speaker, I guess I misjudged by a few metres, and when I landed, I realized just maybe I wasn't yet totally sober. My leg was still attached, I touched my foot, it wasn't broken. Maybe one of the so-called ligaments was torn, I thought, and laughed grubbily to myself.

I decided to become a sailor. On account of the better prospects. No: I decided to finally go find Sigi.

I walked out and caught a taxi to the Tresor.

In the Tresor: no Sigi nowhere.

But there were places where people offered you other things, even beer. I took one and said thanks. I went dancing. I got another beer, drank, danced.

So it was such-and-such night after the parade, and as I was dancing I noticed that I could no longer tell which effect from which drug was taking hold, and this circumstance suited me perfectly. The music gripped me, I liked watching DJ Goodgroove behind the wheels, and I ignored the manifold social events taking place on the dance floor. Suddenly I saw some of the faces around me looking worn out and fucked up and I thought: Tough gig, I probably look just as busted right now too. And I fiddled in my pockets, took something out, to make excessively precise observations or even note down ridiculous thoughts.

Occasionally I would go out and walk around in the garden.

I wandered around.

The morning was dawning, I was glad.

I thought: About time. I looked at my watch. I sat on a bench, leaned on the wall, and smoked.

I decided to drive back to Suicide, right then, to Helli's gig, when was it he was playing there?

I walked over the scrunching gravel.

There, all at once, was my Sigi standing before me,

amusingly some ten times more twatted than I.

It was Monday morning, just before six, and at eleven something our plane was taking off for Ibiza.

III

DESTROYED

'We'll never stop living this way.'

This time I'm doing it differently and I'm telling everyone what I'm writing. This little thing, quick and nasty.

About us.

About the nightlife and all.

Ali: 'Really? Am I in it too?'

'Of course.'

I said this three years ago, wait, no, more than three years ago. Since three years ago, I've been telling everyone who asks me what I'm writing right now: Yeah, I –

Fucked up scene. Pathetic.

Once upon a time there was a little naked earlobe that lay hidden quite softly on two not yet totally naked very cute little labia.

Re-membering for-bidden – sung, naturally, by Die Prinzen, to the melody of their kissing song.

Can you feel it?

Sweetheart.

I thought, now everything will be totally cool. Did you feel that or think that, too?

Aesthetic theory is valid when it examines the interior problems of the artwork.

Textstandstill.

Plotstandstill. – Timestandstill. – Agony.

Confrontations with the ego structure you wouldn't wish on your worst enemy.

Last respects.

1. NEXT NIGHTS

but they want do away with each other.

The stranger stands big, dark, and sinister on the corner, by the tall trees where the park starts or stops on the edge of town. It's night-time now. And it's got cold.

The man is waiting there. He's looking at the ground in front of him, looking at the time. His face is glowing wet and sallow. His mouth is hanging lopsided. And his jawbones grate senselessly, empty.

The man is uneasy. He's walking back and forth.

Two steps back, two steps forwards.

Outside at the airport.

The car stops, Schütte gets out. The passenger side window rolls down, a couple of words are exchanged, Schütte gives the driver a note, stands up, turns around, and looks at his watch.

It's just before nine.

Schütte enters Frankfurt airport, main terminal.

You hear the airport ambience.

Chatting,

Whirring,

Calling and addressing,

Dialogue in snatches.

Schütte looks around, sees the telephone, and walks up to the telephone.

In the hotel hallway. Schütte knocks thrice on the door of Room 24. He enters the darkened room. He sits down with the others, takes cocaine, and lies on the bed. He stares up at the ceiling.

Just before.

Schütte is walking down the hall. The door to Room 12 is open two feet. Bright light emerges from inside. He stops and looks through the crack. On the bed, a girl is lying on her belly.

Schütte lies on his back in bed.

The falconer and the DJ-actress are in the midst of a light conversation. About hair colour. The woman unbuttons her trousers, pulls her panties down in the front until the man can see her public hair, says 'Look!' and laughs.

Back to the airport, International Arrivals.

Schütte takes a silver cigarette case from his jacket, pops it open, it's empty. He looks around, then walks up to an elegant businesswoman leaning on a pillar.

She looks at him.

Him: 'Totally lame come-on. My cigarettes are gone. Might I perhaps ask you – '

'Naturally.'

She passes him her pale Philip Morris box, gives him a light, and nods to his thanks without looking back up. Then she leans back on the pillar and looks into the book she is reading.

Schütte laughs, thanks her again, she looks up and laughs too.

The flap display.

Click-clack of letters and numbers.

Ibiza: Delayed.

The Ibiza flight is running sixty minutes behind.

Schütte tosses his cigarette, strips off his jacket, takes off his sunglasses, and palms his face. Then he goes back towards the main hall.

He walks to the newspaper shop on the corner.

To the register.
'48 please.'
'Here you are.'
'Would you like a bag?'
'A bag would be super.'
'Here you go.'
'Oh, and give me another box of HBs.'

Schütte sits down at a corner table at the Bar Metropolitan, orders a drink, and leafs through the American and English magazines he's purchased.

He looks at the time, counts, and goes back to the phone.

In the hotel, the falconer picks up the receiver, the telephone has just rung.

Next to him the has-been provincial promoter is sitting on the edge of the double bed and passing the short-haired blonde woman from before a metal tube. She bends over the coffee table and sucks cocaine in through her nostrils.

The room is dark, the curtains are drawn, a black T-shirt hangs over the lamp on the nightstand in the one corner.

The woman hands the little tube to Wurzburg's second-most-important flyer distributor, he hands it to the pierced dude no-one there knows, the pierced dude hands it to the guy from Pure, and the guy from Pure to Pia, who gives it to Jale etc. etc.

The Falconer's hung up.

It's quiet.

It is really very quiet now.

No-one says anything.

Silence, white tense silence, reigns over the room.

Schütte is standing in the airport at a public phone surrounded by a Plexiglas shell.

Schütte has hung up mid-call and chooses the next number in his head.

The ringing phone belonging to Marc is lying on the coffee table in the villa in Ibiza.

The table looks like that famous Damien Hirst sculpture entitled: I WANT TO SPEND THE REST OF MY LIFE EVERYWHERE, WITH EVERYONE, ONE TO ONE, ALWAYS, FOREVER, NOW.

Amid empty glasses and full ashtrays

ripped cigarette boxes and a credit card,

a telephone card,

a rolled-up banknote,

beer cans,

pale papers

and a baggie filled with grass, lies the phone.

No music, soft murmurs in the background.

But the phone doesn't move.

Schütte waits, listens.

Hears the message: 'The number you have reached is temporarily unavailable.'

Schütte hangs up. He waits for the cheep from the phone card, takes it out of the slit, sticks it in his jacket and puts his sunglasses back on.

He goes to the taxi rank and gets in the back of the first one. He says: 'Arabella Grand Hotel, please.' Then he lights a cigarette and leans back.

The radio's playing. The driver stinks.

Day three.
'I'm so excited.'
We cross the border.

Frankfurt's streets and schools, Sunday afternoon.
The city's empty.
The taxi drives in. Schütte smokes.
The taxi stops at a red light. A pregnant woman bends down into a poison-yellow pram.

All thoughts are wicked thoughts.

Schütte sits in the airplane, sleeps. The stewardess wakes him and gives him a customs form.
New York.
Schütte is standing in line in front of immigration.
He is waiting in the customs line. He reaches the end and is supposed to open his bags.
How much money does he have with him?
A Grandmaster Flash track is playing.

Another city.
Paris. Paderborn. Emden.
While eating, after the show, in the little artists' pub, Schütte is sitting between two women. Both are touching him. One on the knee, the other has her hand resting on his back.
The women are both drunk. The younger one is

really nice.

She asks Schütte to go back to the hotel with her. Then they lie there in bed. All of a sudden, Schütte is too shy for her.

'Just do it,' she says.

They sleep together.

The next morning, the hotel concierge calls, curses.

In the English Garden.

The man from before talks to a dealer, gives him money. The dealer is a North African and he's still got two nuggets on him. The three of them vanish, the fat guy's got to wait.

First he stands there calm, then he gets nervous, walks back and forth.

Rick and the women leave the English Garden.

Rick: 'There's Ken!'

Ken: 'What brings you here?'

'We were just at the monopteros. You?'

'I'm waiting for my dealer.'

'Sounds good.'

The women say goodbye. Rick goes with Ken.

The dealers come back. Rick orders another gram. Counts. When there's two of you, waiting is no big deal.

Then they drive to Janet's. A long, really wicked night begins.

In front of the Arabella Grand Hotel. Schütte pays the taxi driver and goes inside.

'Wet your whistle, I'll be right back.'

He stands with his back to the lift, waits. Behind him the bell rings. He turns around, gets in, and goes up to the eleventh floor.

He goes down the hall, past the doors.

He enters Room 1112.

Schütte enters Room 1124. The room is full of faces, half of them he's never seen. And yet it's his room.

He talks with the falconer.

They talk about the red bag that didn't show up.

Schütte lies flat on the bed and looks up at the ceiling.

Empty thoughts revolve emptily in his head.

He gets up, grabs the telephone, and calls Marc's mobile again.

But the mobile is still turned off.

Schütte is sitting back at the corner table of the Bar Metropolitan. He's drinking a whiskey, smoking, and reading the big Jay Leno cover story in *Interview*. Then he looks through the other magazines.

Loaded, *Attitude*, *Arena*, *Details*, *i.-D.*, and *Face*.

Schütte reads the drug bits from a cover story on drugs in *Melody Maker*.

He keeps looking at the time.

He scribbles something on the napkin.

He counts and goes back to International Arrivals.

The woman from before is no longer there.

The Ibiza flight has landed.

The first travellers come through.

Schütte keeps his eyes peeled for the red bag.

But the red bag doesn't appear. Schütte waits.

Then at last the last Ibiza traveller arrives, passes through, and still the bag isn't there.

Schütte goes downstairs to Checkers.

Schütte walks up to the door of XLarge on Lafayette Street. Michael Diamond approaches him, walks past him. Schütte goes inside.

He introduces himself, is told to go in the back. Negotiations are done. They talk numbers, money, delivery costs.

Schütte talks and talks.

Abstract business, different dimensions.

Schütte says bye, flags down a taxi, and has them take him to the Holiday Inn in Chinatown.

He walks to the first-floor lounge, orders a drink, and then goes to use the phone.

In the bathroom in the club.

They do cocaine. They go back to the bar and order beers. They drink and smoke. They just stand there, without even really looking around.

It flickers and thunders. Light and fog. Ice.

Nothing else.

Schütte walks through the downstairs hall of the airport.

Neon effects. Dim colours.

People, doors, signs, turnoffs all around.

Schütte wanders through the halls and hallways.

Schütte's got lost.

In the underground garage, the falconer is sitting behind

the wheel of his own parked car, an older Audi 1000, and waiting.

He watches the door.

In front of the door at Checkers.

The doorman greets Schütte with a handshake and says, 'There you are.'

'Hey.'

'I thought you all were waiting at the Arabella.'

'Yeah, no. Ken ever show up?'

'Supposedly.'

'For real?'

Schütte goes inside and walks through the club.

No doubt, it is the age of the last simulations.

Schütte meets Tiermann and they walk to the bathroom together, walk into a stall together, and do cocaine.

They stand there a moment.

Then dump out some more.

They go to the bar by the DJ booth. They greet various people. Schütte finds out the falconer was asking about him.

Tiermann gets an attack of the jabbers. Now he's blabbing on to Schütte.

Schütte feels close to Tiermann.

Feels bothered by him.

Doesn't care.

He's ashamed.

He sees white scurf in the corner of Tiermann's mouth. The observation suddenly takes on monstrous dimensions.

Dreadful.

Schütte wipes the corner of his mouth clean. Once more. Tiermann is loggorheic.

Schütte makes a brief comment, walks away.

He asks different people about Ken. He goes to the bar in the side room and orders whiskey this time. He hears the words:

'On ice.'

He laughs. He looks at the time.

The individual bits of the plot strike him as excessively hacked up, too isolated, and their significance thereby traumatized in an almost absurdly logical way. He drinks down his whiskey.

A shudder reflex shudders Schütte.

A laughing reflex follows.

Schütte walks through the bar. They are raging in front of him, the last of the faithful, to themselves, every man for himself.

Just lovely.

He goes back to the bathroom, waits, because all the stalls are full. Keith comes in. He invites Keith, they go together into a newly opened stall and do more cocaine.

Now Schütte is feeling good.

He leaves the club.

Back through the calm, now splendidly lit halls and hallways painted in cool fluorescent colours. He opens a door and takes the stairs up.

The giant hall he's now crossing, totally still.

All the people totally clear, totally precise.

Completely mad.

Madness, truth, the entire choreography.

He enjoys his derangement.

He sits in the back of a taxi, says: 'Back, please.'
    The taxi driver says back where.

Back to the front of the Arabella Grand Hotel.
    Schütte looks with bug eyes, counts, totally concentrated. He rides the lift down to the basement.
    In the hotel garage he walks between the parked cars as fevered as possible towards something.
    He looks for a quiet corner.
    He peeks around.
    He squats down and sprinkles a thin line of cocaine on his cigarette box.
    The box with the cocaine is lying in front of him on the ground.
    He stands and reaches in his pocket for a banknote.
    He looks around again, and then, as he rolls up the banknote, squats down in front of the cigarette box.
    Then he does the cocaine.
    Very nice.

In his observations of the fucked up nature of the scene, Schütte is allowing a certain indulgence to prevail, appropriate just here and now, as he sees it.

He is standing in the lift, alone.
    Brass, gold, glass, mirror, light.
    The trip up to the 11th floor lasts longer than expected.
    He gets out. He walks down the hall.
    He looks for Room 24.
    He goes back to the lift, studies the arrows and

numbers.

He walks off again. He reads the room numbers: 8, 9, 10.

He stands in front of Room 12 and knocks.

With the doorman, in front of the club.

'Thought you all were in Munich already.'

'We're all still at the Arabella.'

'Have fun.'

'Thanks.'

They are sitting in the ride, a lux rental van.

The vehicle is in an empty car park on the edge of town in front of some supermarket somewhere.

There's like four of them there.

They sit there, take drugs, and chat.

Ernst Jünger, Jackson Pollock, Dostoevsky, and so forth.

After one, two hours, Schütte gets out, walks to the grass border, bends over, and pukes.

Then he wipes his mouth and walks back to the ride.

Maybe that last beer wasn't the best idea. Or maybe it was?

Schütte talks.

The young, ambitious, very successful businessman, good looking, dressed to the nines, rich, popular, clever, sexy, has been expanding in all kinds of directions in recent months.

Fashion, text, women.

In the last half-hour things have started getting out of hand. Call in to Cape Town. Flight to Las Vegas. Brief session in the Hamburg Tunnel, behind the rear office.

The textile producer has got a title.

Call to Prinz the lawyer.

Prinz is the subject of an appalling defamation campaign, which may be the doing of Markwort from *Focus*. The *Focus* editor Christian Gottwald is asking such stupid questions.

Frontpage and *Spex* want to do big title stories.

Good.

Then it's a game of roulette.

The ball's rolling. Ha.

Bet high and bet fast, that's what it's about. A kind of pool of ideas, with high number rotation, always in motion.

Everyone in suits, snazzy.

'Any chance you could maybe come through with five thousand marks for me?'

The ideal activities.

The very real holes in the balance sheet.

'I am not aware of what you're referring to, sir.'

Call to Philip Morris.

Call to Camel.

Call to Red Bull.

Probably they all sleep at night, right?

When you plug a hole, you make new holes. Some kind of snare seems to be drawing closed.

Obviously totally ridiculous in essence.

Intervention at the European History Court in Prague.

Richard II, Maximilian I, the House of Schwarzenbeck, Wolfsegg, Altensam, and everything connected thereto, the assembled European nobility, Wirr, Dark, Rutte, and everyone else step forward and declare themselves firmly in solidarity with the complaint.

The setting is sombre somehow.

The money's gone. The accounts are closed.

The air thins.

New ideas have long been in the works.

The waiter comes: 'Did you want the bill?'

'Put it on Room 1124 please.'

'Room 1124, of course.'

The chick from Strada signs her name Schütte and gets up.

Schütte and the chick from Strada in Room 1112.

They do cocaine.

Intrigued, they roll around on top of one another.

Schütte sleeps in.

The chick walks into the salon, meets a friend there. They order a little something to eat.

'You happen to know what time it is?'

'No idea.'

Schütte wakes up and walks over to Room 24.

Unchanged scenery there, unchanged constellation.

Schütte calls Marc's mobile again.

This time it even rings.

Schütte: 'It's ringing.'

Marc's mobile is lying next to the pool this time under a towel.

The white villa in Ibiza, the swimmers, the villa from afar in the hilly island green.

No-one hears the phone.

Next day.

Back at International Arrivals at Frankfurt airport.
We make it through customs no problem.
Schütte's already waiting for us.
Marc was too late telling him about our delay.
Sorry.
No probs.
The bag gets handed over in Marc's car and opened.
Then there's money.
Don't mention it.
Have a good one.
You too, now.

Then we drive off back to Munich.

2. LITTLE LETTERS TO ISABELLE

You're always too busy
making new mistakes to worry
about the old ones.

ATTENSHUN. ATTENSHUN. The teachers have lost their minds. Burn down all the schools.

SCHÜTTE is sitting in the Bar Metropolitan and reading the Chemical Brothers story in *Face 200*. He could have easily overlooked it, given the title. But the story's not about the goofy eponymous band, it's about Irvine Welsh and Shaun Ryder.

The night before, after the MTV Awards, Shaun Ryder unintentionally wound up doing some kind of cocaine cut with speed. Afterwards he spent a quick quarter-hour in the hotel getting thrashed by his girlfriend. And now – anyway this is how Andrew Harris, the writer from *Face* tells it – it's 10.25 a.m. and he's apparently walking into the shady bar all beat up and Irvine Welsh is sitting there with his Bloody Mary in front of him. Irvine Welsh puts down his drink, stands up a bit, and greets Shaun Ryder.

The conversation that follows is a highly entertaining mix of subjects, problems, and objects, just as you'd expect from the two of them.

They talk about records, drugs, films, music, and writing, about their output and their drives, their thoughts and their actions. Could even be about Plato, too, the parts concerned with the fundamentality and the bandwidth of the subject, and the factors of casualness and exactitude.

I tell Tom immediately.

We're standing in the Six Pack in Cologne and debating aloud about the dust-ups the two of us got into in print in the weeks before. I'm at the part about self-criticism. Is there anything more mendacious than self-criticism? Anything smugger? Self-criticism: that's not even a thing, that's a contradiction in terms, there is hardly anything more contradictory, that is a unique moral absurdabsurdity, if not indeed an absoluteabsurdity. *Spex* is oozing with it. Ugly, wrong.

And in this context, I thus quote this quote from Irvine Welsh, about making mistakes, about new mistakes, which don't even leave you the time to deal with old mistakes, because you have to constantly make new mistakes. That is the normal and reasonable way of practising self-criticism: making new mistakes. That's what I say to Tom.

THE BIGGEST VICTIM in the struggles of recent years to reclaim the political realm – and under friendly fire, so to speak, under the brutal continuous firepower of morality – is humour. Saturday night can't be an excuse forever.

Humour in the sense of the completely automatic, as it were instinctive mental pleasure taken in the struggle of mental objects, contradictions, ambiguities, exaggerations, vulgarities, and their endless, brutal wrangling with one another.

Take Diedrich, writing about Kippenberger's politics five minutes after Kippenberger's death: Oops. But it doesn't hurt anyone, it is actually even objectively quite silly.

200

STOP. Don't read this. This is obscene.

POP KOMM COLOGNE. The legally responsible editor-in-chief of the esteemed American underground lefty rag *Sex and Matter*, Chris Turk, is drunk. He is talking with a prospective freelance collaborator who is similarly tipsy. They take aspirin together, cut up, naturally. They talk themselves into a rage over politics and controversy. They get each other. A moment of eroticism and perhaps even sexuality comes into play. In order better to clarify the various questions thus brought to the fore, they resolve to go on discussing things in Turk's hotel room, which is nearby. In the room, after a brief shame-pause of silence, Turk leaps on the prospective freelancer. She defends herself, explains this wasn't what she had in mind. Turk flies into a rage, bolts the door, and there occurs a – however you look at it – very scandalous event, essentially one of an extremely sexist sort. Rather dreadful for all involved.

The next day Turk writes a detailed apology to a writer of a letter to the editor who has reproached him for his politically incorrect, thoughtless use of the word 'Turk'. Turk apologizes for everything.

SCHÜTTE RINGS UP and asks: So are vice, villainy, debasement, and repulsiveness not just as normal as everything non-repulsive and good, and all the striving for the latter constantly taking place? Are not the exorcistic excesses of consequent apologies, redress, and political correctness and the overtone of self-righteousness and arrogance they generate not a bald-faced shameless affront to the entire moral mixture of realities of which reality is constituted? And where is the concrete individual life which, being so righteous, may claim for itself the right to eternally dictate right and wrong to everyone else in the world?

Huh?

Isn't that what we're talking about? And if not, what?

AT THE NEXT TABLE OVER the elegant businesswoman, shortly before addressing Schütte, reads an article in the *Berliner Zeitung* by former *FAZ Feuilleton* editor Gustav Seibt.

Gustav Seibt – not to be confused, moreover, with the young nobleman of a similar name, whose weapon taken down from the curtain rod earlier came from one of the houses in *Thomas Bernhard's Houses* – is writing today about yesterday's premiere of Brecht's *Decision* at the Berliner Ensemble.

TO NONE OTHER THAN THE WASHED-UP PROVINICAL PROMOTER Seibt's wife explains exhaustively, later that night at the hotel bar, in the presence of Giulietta, the little raver girl from before, that this is the fascinating thing about Brecht, the longing for the collective. Not the result, but the interest; the direction of the direction of the gaze and not the standpoint. The political MOTOR IMPULSE then, which in the poetry –

Both are equally hollow: the deed-prison of the Yes and the reflex-No eternally in the thoughtprison of the No.

TO LEARN FROM BRECHT, then, that would mean – well, what?

Debate with Anselm on the phone. Discussion of the premiere of the new play, JEFF KOONS. It's about the political aspects of artistic praxis in a more or less classic

202

artist-drama, amid the political conditions of today, so *after 1989*. Whatever all that is supposed to mean.

KRYPSE-RULE: A text should have no secrets. It should silence nothing it knows about itself. This maxim is helpful in proceeding with purpose and staying on the defence against any possible obscurantist poetastery and illusory depths that might creep in.

Say everything you know.

Clear and simple, just like it is.

That's not so hard, though. The eternal question is simply: when, where, and how can this EVERYTHING be said precisely, in which portions and particles, and in which setting. And how, if possible, can it emerge practically automatically, as if it were uttering itself. Without compulsion, unforced then, without violating the rules of tact and discretion that prevail within a text.

But: What kind of rules are these? How do you go about apprehending this? It changes constantly. With every sentence, with every new word.

In what way does a given text reconstitute a society? What attitudes, emotions, diction, theoretical models, linguistic partnerships, and words compose society in the abstract, the societal-intellectual character embodied in a given text? And what are the rules that govern it?

We want to examine such poetological questions translated into the realm of music, that's what I discuss with Max in Studio 5.5.

THE DAY BEFORE I MEET Anne in front of the door to The Lounge. The mood is super, earlier we'd been at Ulf's place celebrating Moritz's twenty-seventh birthday with all these writers from the *Süddeutsche* feuilleton, from *Jetzt*, and from *SZ-Magazin*, and other friends from the adjacent worlds of film, photo, music, and nightlife.

Only Maxim Biller, who would automatically have been there three years ago, couldn't make it. He must still have been brooding about his forthcoming column. Some vulgarity must have not yet been sufficiently vulgar and needed to be sanded down to a very fine point. Will certainly be highly interesting next time, too.

This motley birthday society then drove in various factions to the Lounge with the Saturday night war cry of 'Extreme Lounging'. I went for example with the so-called bike. Went inside, said hi to Michi Reinboth, found the brachial drum and bass that was playing extremely cool, I ordered a cola from Martina and was elated to run into Susi, whom I hadn't seen for what seemed like an eternity.

As I said, dope vibe. What happened then: I walked downstairs to see where the others were and ran into Anne at the door. Just before I was telling Claudius Seidl about the unmitigated disaster of the two Annes' Luhmann article that had appeared a few days ago. Total incomprehension from Claudius. What do you mean? It was cool. Then Claudius had to go.

And my remaining arguments, which I had not yet conveyed to him, I now vomited out without warning and in a frankly absurdly direct manner straight into the face of the speechless and shocked Anne now standing there before me.

Extreme Lounging. Nasty business.

I wasn't wrong, actually. But a person can't really just

behave like that. Or can they?

What do you think?

In the meantime, Anne's article about ketamine also came out in *SZ-Magazin*. Even worse. Totally busted: poetry, confusion, journalism. Instead of truth, experience, knowledge, at the very least the richness of scientific knowledge. Nothing at all, just dim-witted poetry album poetry. Truthomitted poetry. The HORROR.

MANI IS STANDING ON THE DANCE FLOOR in the lounge, just then he's got a hat on and is speaking English into the microphone. He holds the microphone out to me, I'm supposed to come up and rap something too. I wouldn't have the least idea what there might be to say. Right here, right now, at the party, in the middle of the club.

Later, at the door: I need to call him tomorrow. He's got to tell me something. OK. It's about the DJ Academy. Mani's on his way out, he'll call back. We talk about the Air Rave. Yes, even the Camel Air Rave alas has gone the way of all flesh. The ultimate grandiose decadent culmination event of Rave Tourism for all present is gone and is never coming back.

Some responsible party has had to give up his responsibility or else just lost the will, some pot of money has been dumped out, some money flow turned off, somebody in some position somewhere has transferred or lost or quit that position by chance. But some new crackpot is already at the ready.

A big shot from Red Bull wants to try something new. There's got to be an ACADEMY, he's heard this from Miami time and again and time and again from other people, so he says: OK, make it happen.

DJ ACADEMY. You in? – Sure, why not? – Well you are the winner of the Red Bull Invitation to the Red Bull DJ Academy, one of fifty out of umpteen-thousands. Bingo.

Beginners' course.

Day 1: What is music anyway? – Listen to different music. How long has there been rhythm? How do you recognize rhythm? Everyone try to imagine music without rhythm. – Afternoon: Learn to count, practise counting beats.

Day 2: Learn to appreciate tempos. – Does the track presently playing have 114, 121, 138, or 154 BPM? Headphones on: is the second track on the headphones slower or faster than the first? Don't ask why, just say: How much? – Play with the pitch control.

Day 3: Learn pitches. Today, the professor has no desire for detailed explanations. Work in silence individually.

Day 4: Practise beat matching. Get the records to the same speeds. Identify the 1 in each track and cross over. The 1 doesn't sound so good, so take the 2 or the 4. Turn the silent record up. And if possible on the 1 of a music-unit of 2 or 4 beats, but it depends on the record, it could also be 2 or 12.

Now: How does it sound? Normally for the first three months: totally off. What came through as rhythmically consonant in the mind in reality doesn't come through at all. – Afternoon: Learn to hear, practise hearing.

Day 5: Objective diagnosis of the mix as it runs – crisis intervention. Both records are playing out loud. But it doesn't sound right. Why? Is one too fast? Which? Or are they both at the same speed, but the rhythm isn't clicking?

Intervention on the basis of the object of diagnosis, renewed objective diagnosis: Does it work now? No. The intervention was a total flop. The slowed down record was limping back behind, now it's not. Attempt at the opposite measure, push it. Result: it's been pushed too far. Etc. etc.

Afternoon: practise the transition between sentimentally and rationally controlled mixing praxis. Figure out for once what is rhythmically off and what's happening, and how you do something about it and why; and next time do everything according to feel. Then try it the other way around.

Day 6: Lessons in adventurism. – Naturally you are a bummy Red Bull Adventurer. But you want to become a cool DJ. That means that with every mix you wager a bit more than you're actually capable of. In winter sports English, you go wild on the slopes but you can't ski straight on the way down. Cool.

But: however wild and adventurous you break into a mix again and again, that is just how SUPER-SCRUPULOUS and auditorially pedantic you need to be, checking whether you've got that wild mix-manoeuvre under control, or whether it's plucked you up and thrown you into the chaotically rhythmic pounding and carnage – and you have to cut it off.

Why? When it's so much fun!

To keep from getting on the listeners' nerves. Get this straight: for you yourself, almost everything you do sounds cool. For others, not necessarily. Always imagine someone listening to the radio who doesn't get the whole background behind the thing and only hears the musical result.

Play with the lightning-fast oscillation between adventure-madness and musical-professional-scrupulousness.

And naturally: party and fuck every night. For that is the central and highest purpose of all academies, congresses, fairs, discussion circles, and readings – political, artistic, automotive, diverting, or scientific, over and above them stands the motto: Mutual inspection of carnal reality, presence, touching, sex.

See above, and – excuse me – especially, naturally, BELOW.

Afterwards practise at home, this time with tape. The tapes say actually: In all truth what you thought was a transition in the heat of battle of the act of mixing is just repulsive bungling. This is where you learn admiration for the craft of this art, the agility, otherwise you'll never be a DJ. Athletic ambition awakens. Now the first little gigs must come, otherwise what's the point, DJing is a social affair. Is there anyone at all who doesn't enjoy learning this?

Listen. Look.

And all other thoughts vanish in this sort of receptively grasping reflexivity.

INTERVIEW. What is the techno experience you would least wish to do without?

This completely new hearing of the everyday world's noise an excessive concentration on music engenders.

THIS IS THE SUMMER when I traipsed at least three times a week through the little streets of Glockenbach to the Optimal, most often with a book in hand, most often that summer Luhmann's *Art of Society*, to –

'Hey, Lester, what's up?'

– listen to records, the newest, the old, the older, the cool, the wack. All kinds of records.

To hang out in the record store.

How cool: listening to basically all the new releases. Pursuing this or that historical question, maybe even listening through an entire label's catalogue. And in this way over time automatically becoming an increasingly nervous judgement machine. Recognizing, ridiculing the excessive tension of this nervousness, relinquishing it, struggling against it, and having fun with everything.

Letting it emerge as an autonomous judgement event, a judgement process, an evaluative crisis of judgement, and letting the raging battle between equivocation and stubbornness, between knowledge and mental emptiness, just happen, without intervening: a bit strenuous, the passivity method, doesn't always work, rather seldom, really.

This weakness is called character. Normally that doesn't get you so far in life, because the uncertainty and unpredictability it harbours place too heavy a burden on the social process. Then eventually position comes to stand in for judgement. And every artwork becomes a throwback to the radicality, autonomy, and openness of the individuation experiences in the judgement of the early years.

I gather notes under the title: 'On the blessing of poverty.'

FANTASTIC PARALIPOMENA. The concept of the artwork implies that of success. But failed artworks are artworks in spite of everything, just less beautiful. The middling is not the worst, rather most often the normal. A kind of horizon of art.

On the word NO in Adorno.

HENCE A POLITICS, which begins supersimply just with oneself at home in the house. And at the same time with the way one gives oneself bodily, as an I, to the others. This is where the social begins.

Benevolence is irritating.

Arguments are irritating.

Apparently symbolic politics is irritating. And brutal to boot. So brutal that –

Albert advises: Strike out the things that are personally hurtful.

That's a good idea.

Thanks a lot.

EDUCATION MEASURES should incidentally also be: interventionist, frightening, unexpected, capricious, nasty. Like most things that happen. That is what makes one amenable to learning, through facts. Man is not so easily educable, is only with difficulty educable, through arguments.

Oh, no, no thanks, you think to yourself, the harder others try to educate you. And the more they repeat some educational goal, the more they justify it, the greater the desire grows to do the very opposite. Just for a laugh. To take the piss out of the educators a bit.

THE FUNCTION OF ARGUMENT is moreover not – even when arguments themselves like to behave this way – to convince someone else of something. In reality arguments give you clarity about the rationale of your own intuitions.

The more confused thinking is, the broader it deploys its argumentation in general. And as its argumentativeness increases, the shell that seals it off from the apprehension of other ideas almost inevitably grows more impenetrable. Those who argue most fiercely are almost always interested exclusively in constructing their own often honestly quite miserable argumentative structure. That lends something childish to professional posturing as a whole.

Posts and positions. The *Academy*. Applying for posts and taking positions. Pay grades for adjunct, assistant, full. *Illegitimate* fields.

All that is bullshit, people.

I FEEL

everyone should be allowed to do what they want. I want to do what I want too.

Take drugs as much as you want.

Go out whenever you want.

Listen to music as loud as you want.

Read what you want.

And work when, where, and how you like.

And love?

3. THROW DOWN RIP UP FLIP OUT

and hope that some of you
will carry these experiments further
and will come up with
something new.

Then it was autumn.

The great rain came, and the leaves withered drab on the trees. It was the year after A-levels, the year before A-levels, the year before or after the first, second, or third book, stranded somewhere in the mid-eighties.

Karl had talked to me after a concert outside at the Theaterfabrik. No-one can remember what concerts we used to go to then. Before Public Enemy and Bad Brains? It was Modern Talking time, it was leather jacket time, and I was standing on the stairs up to the left, and during the encore I saw how Karl glanced at me – and – this was the only way you could see it – made eyes at me. Sigi stood next to him, long blond hair, the ersatz Don Johnson from Untergiesing.

I was annoyed at being pestered, talked to, pressured, having to take these cute blond types with me in the car back into the city. I sat there spiteful behind the wheel. Karl said this and that. And suddenly it occurred to me: right, even here, I was the dude who had written *Insane*. That's even more horrid, that really is just idiotic. What a horrid beginning for this story.

We saw each other a little while later, maybe one, two, three, four weeks afterward, back at the Purple Rain Bar in the Baaderstrasse, where I was drinking with Floli. Karl and Sigi, Wolli and Bernd, Ladi and Stefan and a couple of handballers and a couple of burnouts.

212

And this time there was a BOOM. Right away there was a high, the first complete communal high, brotherhood, brothers hanging together. And this first night I find myself sitting there with Karl somewhere on the edge of the floor, basically hand in hand, inspired and delighted by each another and infatuated and saying nothing, totally drunk.

So it was.

And we took it from there.

Wolli had shorn off his hair and was one of the first guys outside the hardcore gay scene to rock this hard femme bare skull like an immoderately explicit cry for sex, a signal made abstruse by his slightly eccentric shy self-consciousness, shamelessly lascivious, directed at men and women alike from around the way.

He was sitting with me in the car, the others were already gone, we were alone. He was talking about swimming and playing his music. And I thought, now he's going to touch me, or I'm going to touch him. And I didn't get that. What's he want then? We stood in front of his door, talked. I had shut off the motor. Suddenly it was silent, and no-one said anything, and nothing happened.

When I came back from Paris, the city had changed. The city: the nightlife. My substitute service period was over, and now things were supposed to take off somehow. But how?

In fact, when you focus your blurry eyes intently on the common vanishing points of the almost daily conversations – in the baths, at the dance clubs, at the Parkcafé and the P1, at the New York and the Pimpernel and the attendant beer drinking and Rüscherl excess and high strung shrillness – inevitably it turned around about POLITICS.

Funny enough: impossible to reproduce. The bygone sincerity, the real monumentality of the political, the openness of the future of a very particular individual life in its submission to chance, utopias, the contemporary private politics of lived praxis in countless tiny *Realpolitik* decisions: reproducible neither in scenes nor images, strangely, more or less immune to reconstruction.

THE LIE – you can find that in big grey letters on every page, wherever you look for it. There is a gesture of thoroughgoing minimization – you need only read Wildenhain – and a simultaneously romantic-kitsch tone of exaggeration – see Geißler – that transforms the revolutionary through contemptible mendacity into a pseudo-affair of renunciation and struggle, sacrifice and duty.

The truth is it never was and never has been that way. A representation in conformity with reality – the entire confusion and simultaneity of all contradictory motives and moral aspects – the emotional triumphalism of goodness and the embarrassment of that moment of realization of the rectitude of one's political vision – cannot be depicted from the perspective of the actors and the fighters, the heroes, no matter how broken. And even Peter Weiss's *Aesthetics* is not free from all this, from this tone-and-sentimentality problem, even it has not truly been able to solve this problem in a satisfactory way.

It was *Tempo*-time. And however much we felt tormented by the monthly appearances of this entire *Tempo*-world, by the real power of this world, which *Tempo* had not so much invented as portrayed in an ideal way, thereby

214

amplifying it the way a good magazine should, tormented too by the authentic *Tempo*-world as it actually existed
and functioned – however tormented we felt, we felt lib-
erated as well. We had *Tempo* to thank for our political
opinions, for our fundamental stance of opposition.

And we knew it. Without *Tempo*, our non-*Tempo* existence would have been unable to take part in the *Tempo*
world, and there wasn't a touch of naivety to all that. The
ambivalences and absurdities were totally evident, were
part of our political activity, could not and should not be
idealized away. It was the eighties, not the sixties. It was
the most contrary and most political, the most radical
and rich, the most unstruggling decade of decades, even
in its culmination in 1989, of this entire goddamned
century.

That was a rough ride. I was glad when it was finally
over.

We wanted to learn again from the RAF then. But not
in terms of action. It was about the arguments. We studied the texts. Wolli wrote a big research paper about the
language of the RAF. He even went to Wiesbaden and
interviewed there one of those Federal Criminal Police
specialists. The idea was to depart from the tone of the
commandos' explanations, from the speech acts they
perpetrated and the representational aspects of their arguments, and to obtain through this as realistic an image
as possible of the revolutionaries' everyday life as such.
Then, compare that with the earlier RAF texts, with the
very first ones, with the horrible late letters from the
Info System.

Today, when the RAF is finally beginning to turn back
to its origins as a wild pop phenomenon that captured the
heart of the Republic and indeed even transformed it in

quite a revolutionary way, you can hardly imagine how hard it actually was back then to recognize the process of collapse in the faith in the RAF; you couldn't really grasp the real decline at the core of the political utopia, the deception of the shocking, increasingly granular militarism of the increasingly senseless murders, you can hardly resuscitate in your mind how you bristled at having to admit to yourself, at long last, the politically fucked up-ness of this path and its obsession with the highest ideals.

So I resurfaced from this work in the end, indescribably fucked up myself, through and through. I went to Berlin, back to Paris, to Frankfurt, to Kassel, to Hamburg, to Spain, to Mallorca. '88. The grimmest, most dreadful, most horrible summer of my life.

I went back to Munich.

The gang of boys became a group of young men. O misery of all biographies. When the paths clear up and everyone becomes what he is and was from the beginning. How everything sharpens and clarifies, turmoil turns to order, ambiguities dissipate, the immeasurable dissolves and turns into a life, a merely human life.

And yet: I had long been broken, wrecked, and melancholic enough to find all of that as it should be. I also saw in Boris Becker's great struggle to become an adult the coolest consequence of the heavenliness of youth.

The group's inner equilibrium turned dynamic and shifted several times, the defined proximity of individuals and others had crossed and crisscrossed, reciprocal alienations and disappointments, rivalries and self-rediscoveries remixed the quintet thoroughly several times over. That was the cool thing, actually. The more clearly the individuals emerged, the less recognizable the status of the gang as a whole became.

Slowly we grew into something almost like a factor in the city, a nucleus of the night, a core of virulence, that would change the Munich night.

Nine years later, this story can be known and told through the form and mood of the great mafia films. Rise and fall. The fall of the House of Corleone.

In unglamorous terms: a film like *Donnie Brasco*.

In power and banality terms, and the terms of obtuse violence of tragedy: something like *Casino*.

And you actually think – or does it just seem that way? – that because there is a pattern, if only BECAUSE it is so blatantly obvious, that you are not and can't be and will not become a victim.

But you are wrong.

We used to sit with the Italians on the corner of Fraunhofer and Müllerstrasse almost every afternoon before our so-called shift, we'd buy the early edition of the next day's paper if the vendor happened to come by, we'd read the paper and talk. About yesterday, about today, about the business. The business was a little candy kiosk, a little coatroom to the left of the entrance to Babalu. The business was Thursdays, that was when Wolli took his turn running Babalu, began staging Techno Thursdays on his own account.

The business was the status of the night ever renewed from one day to the next: other cliques, other bars, other parties and celebrations. But the idea of the Corleone firm, its actual secret business purpose, was the monetization of an abstract capital: FUN AND FAME.

We'd already got a certain rep, a certain respect among the other nightmakers: as sots. This is how the real fairy tales of real nights everywhere begin. With such-and-such a person getting brutally hammered on such-and-such a date; drunk under the table at such-and-such a place; totally hammered and saying such-and-such to such-and-such a person.

What now?

Us. A new US.

And anyway that is in itself the eternally valid, resounding, and absolutely peremptory argument: the newness of the new, the usness of us.

You can't invent, fake, make up, plan this kind of lunacy. Blind longing, venturesome mood, spurred by the completely appropriate disdain, for more power and more exhilaration, more fun and more sex than the rest of the world, these pirates invade collectively, and are the bosses, the bosses of excess.

Who's that, who are they?

And everywhere whispers and murmurs: the House of Corleone. They're coming. Here they come, watch out.

Boozing a path of devastation through the clubs, that was a question of honour. And the next weekend we're back out drinking again, making short work of whatever gets in our way. Drinking a path of devastation straight across Germany, from Munich, Frankfurt, Cologne, to Hamburg, and back. That was the idea, shudder to think: drinking Germany dry. They already know us back home. Along with all the casual flings with casual chicks, birds, and skirts. And the eternally recapped eternal clichés, over and over, of course.

Babe, get naked, I gotta tell you something. – If you're

feeling froggy, jump.

Karl and Berndt had made friends with this psychiatry professor from Haar who saw himself as an Achternbusch type, a guy who drank wheat beer and spoke in Bavarian, a true rustic type. Used to shout out his greetings to me like so. Skeeved me out.

One time we were sitting in a beer garden off in the sticks, in Ambach I think it was, I had gone swimming with Bernd and then went along with him to meet up with Karl, and here was this weird psychiatry professor sitting across from me and I couldn't give him the slip. And he goes talking on and on to me IN BAVARIAN. I can't even express how much I hate Bavarian and every other dialect for that matter. What crass nonsense, a dipshit psychiatry professor of all things trying to redeem himself by speaking Bavarian.

This was the kind of guy Karl and Bernd were making friends with then. Gives you something to think about.

And for that very reason things got heated as we kept drinking. Bernd was such a puss anyway. And Karl was slow on the uptake and the fact is, he sometimes failed to catch on.

But that's no good. That doesn't do it.

There exists a compulsion to drink and be present in the nightlife, especially among such informal groups and cliques. Whoever doesn't come through, whoever doesn't come through regularly and isn't willing to get hammered right away loses his permission to be with and talk with. Is antisocial. That's just how it is.

All of a sudden, Karl turned into a passionate cinephile. And in Munich, as is well known, that is a very stern, very bitter fraternity. Werkstatt-Kino, Stadtmuseum, preview here, premiere there, late night show at this place, and original versions, I'll have mine with cream, please, thanks. Before you know it, every cinephile, this is the cinephile's utmost duty, has developed a totally crazy super-special-specific interest. And they cultivate this super-special-field passionately and super-seriously. Korean electro-splatter crime flicks, or was it Taiwanese porno animations, but only in black and white?

Nah, only in colour.

In the spring of 1990, not long after the original broadcasts of the East German Round Table – again you had these photo series with fade-in text – *Die Sendung mit der Maus* has been cancelled. We will now continue with the Round Table – just like a few years before when it was: We will now continue with Wimbledon – the new 'Germany' cheer began. Really and truly, I thought I had something in my ear. In each of the gazillion news programmes you would watch every day they'd broadcast these repugnant German flags flapping en masse, then they'd cheer the 'unity' cheer, and it felt like you'd actually landed in an old newsreel with the Big Boss shouting his DOITSCHLANT DOITSCHLANT shout in his Big Boss dialect out to the masses.

Brutal. Too repugnant. Unbearable.

I kept thinking, I've got to get out of here, I can't bear this Germany bullshit anymore, this constant German Germany cheer. The abhorrent *Bild Zeitung* with its dull, dumb, hollow nationalist fever. Hardly a day passed when the printed word didn't literally scream at you from within its black and red and yellow margins. I can no longer write in these conditions, suffused with hatred for this idiotic Hitler language yelling at me incessantly from the TV in the guise of a live, fresh, authentic text.

I remember asking my mother when we were walking through the cemetery whether she heard it, too? Whether for her too this prosody, this croaking broken screaming propaganda tone was as dreadful, as intolerable as the fascist war fever croaking from before?

Again I packed a car full of books and drove to London. What freedom, to be a European. You think you can't take life anymore because of the political-medial fascist terror. And after two hours in an airplane, everything is different, everything. And in England everything is cool. The people, the language, the pirate stations, London. I want to grow old here someday, that's what I kept thinking.

A year passed. But when spring came, I couldn't do it anymore. There was no more turbulence in the air, that earthly, aimless plenitude of longing that always makes me so happy, so mad, in February. And here you're too high up on the high seas in the narrow little ship of England. They have constant storms and such civil people. They have no spring. A shame. But they have the craziest garden programmes on the TV and there are damp green meadows everywhere, the English with their garden-tinkerer-madness comb, caress, discuss, trim and blow. My god, is all that cool.

And so, that summer when I came back from London, the honourable society had moved. Now we always met, almost every single evening, again, before the evening's activities began, at this Italian place in the Kirchenstrasse in Haidhausen.

Wolli was living there. With wife, still no kid.

Wolli had got married.

A nightlife joke via a nightlife wedding had become a completely brutally real authentic reality. Then sofas were purchased, little stools varnished, paintings hung on the walls; photo art beautified formerly beautiful empty spaces everywhere, gimcracks from Japan and London stood on a shelf beneath an ivy-framed mirror in the bathroom next to a box with tampons in such-and-such a size. That, for example, was something about which one would have preferred less exact knowledge.

Here alone there branched off a myriad of truly indescribably nasty bits and teeny tiny atoms of gossip, whole human fates and dramas without end. Naturally we will pass over this dreadful diversion, just as in real life, where we forgo eternally boring into the drastic and the deathly-sad; and so, one night we see each other on the way into pizzeria Quinque Anni, the boss greets Wolli like a boss with a handshake, and on over to the best table. Nice bottle of wine, fresh fish. Thanks a lot.

Your wife coming along?

No, the wife's tired. Women apparently often enjoy getting tired in the evening. Maybe they're making a mistake and working, maybe even during the day.

That can't happen to us. We've got to get sloshed, always, get sloshed on the regular, or drink at the very least, no matter what, we must urgently drink alcohol nonstop and get drunk. Often as possible, hard as possible. The others don't sleep either. Cheers.

What had been pure madness was suddenly a profession. The levity was gone. Talking about others, other cliques, other shows, other clubs and movers and shakers all turned venomous. Droll arrogance mutated into a mere irritable whininess. Now all of a sudden there's something to defend, some stupid rep, a claim, a real or imaginary claim to arrogance.

This guy and that guy hadn't been here or there, didn't have the cred the way we did, the requisite sincerity. The stories they were spreading, they'd ripped all that off.

We would actually talk like that, that fucked up.

But for the time being we still had fun on our side. Same way Wolli and I stood hundreds of hours, hundreds of nights at the door to some dance spot, now we stood hundreds of hours in front of the door to Babalu. And hundreds more in front of Alcatraz and hundreds of thousands in front of Ultraschall. What could be better: you stand in front of the door to the club and the spaces and you talk, you talk about what's really going on.

That's all there is.

There is no yesterday in the life of the night.

Around one thirty, two, once the bill was taken care of, we'd drive in Wolli's yellow Golf and go stick up posters. Through Haidhausen, the University quarter, Schwabing. We put up posters for Wolli's Thursdays and, once a month, for the big Sven Parties.

Wolli had, we all actually laughed at him about this, an exclusive contract, so many thousands paid in advance, to throw a Sven Väth party every month for one year.

What would happen if the parties flopped?

What was this swaggering professional-poser doing with such a contract?

Wolli was somehow sure of himself though.

As a promoter you must have the capacity to consider

the last burnt out bulb as no less important than the half-mark more or less that the parking attendant receives in his wages; must grasp the importance of this very same parking attendant's friendliness and yet manage to give equal weight to the big conceptual questions: what direction the music's taking, the party as a whole, what's happening in the heads of the people on the scene, while at the same time taking an interest in all other possible people, especially those who, for reasons of age, one may not or ought not let into the club.

As a promoter, naturally, you always need new ideas, you must always have a clear and up-to-date notion of what a cool party looks like, what it needs; you must be able to estimate realistically how much it's going to cost, when saving a thousand doesn't matter and when it's a catastrophe; you must be able to negotiate good deals with light and sound rental companies, and even find the right tone to take when the flyer designer is a mega-dunce, the flyer distributor a drunk, and every second bar chick is a junkie.

You have to be a grifter and a hustler, in a way, and at the same time in another way a person money doesn't mean a shit to.

You need a boundless but not tedious interest in other people, in people of all shades and stripes. An almost amoral interest that takes a meeting not immediately in terms of degrees of sympathy and antipathy, but situationally, as an evernew point of departure for your own unreflective – unreflective as possible – reflex reaction.

And you've got to have dreams in which theory appears reasonable and somehow comprehensible as its own social practice.

224

You need to have a seriously cool head and at the same time be twitchy like an aspen leaf in your sensitivity to every minimal communication, every message that arises almost wordlessly from the mass of many raging quickly alternating mini-meetings, from the relentless exchange of words and glances all brought together. You need measureless ambition and a not-give-a-fuckitude that nearly grazes the antisocial; endless pride, and at the same time a sort of bathroom attendant's humility as regards your own existence.

As a promoter you need to be rigid, stubborn, and un-teachable, a visionary; and then capable every evening of being stirred, assured, taught by the numbers, the money brought in, the reception or the sparseness of the public, the way, in a truly visionary way, your own vision is envisioned by the many others it is there to serve.

And Wolli was a promoter in precisely this all-embracing sense.

Besides that, Wolli had an ear for stories. Stories that never had an end. The kind of stories you yourself had experienced, or the kind everyone always tells you. Upshot being he doesn't get on your nerves, you can't help but have fun with this sort of rag-and-bone collector, with the selection, the rubbish-heap of stories that accumulate in such a person. I could spend hours every day listening to the potpourri of texts that get talked through in this way.

We went to every corner of the earth together, from Helsinki to Zagreb to Bali, for no other reason than to party. And we talked endlessly about everything and at the same time kept secret the ever-growing cosmos of all the things we kept secret in the most mutually agreeable way we could.

The Book of Wolli is far from written.

Blowing money was all at once a thing, I mean big time. THE gag. Just before going to sleep at the hotel, totally drunk, of course, urgently order room service right quick, a few hundred marks' worth, slide the card once up and once down. Blabber on and on. And then of course you're sleeping your arse off by the time the food gets there.

Give me a red rose with that, please.

And yet, insensibly, the whole thing started to slowly have something thorny about it.

The big stupid squandering of money, which really was only funny and meaningful as long as the money you burned for the most expensive hotels, the suites and flights, the pointless room service and the bottles of champagne at this or that bar in foreign cities, was money you DIDN'T have, so that burning through money was contempt for money, an immense grotesque mockery.

Now all of a sudden though it was really just a totally serious imbecilic show-off act. You blew your money and thought: Cool, look how pointlessly I'm blowing my money.

Where was the joke? The joke got lost somewhere along the way. Got ground up somewhere, with time, by the years.

The years. Dreadfully the years flowed off downstream. They came and went, and calmly and unspectacularly, unnoticeably performed their steady work of annihilation in people's lives, our lives. It turned to summer, winter came, and all at once the upcoming year was standing at the door.

Hey there! I want in. I want to destroy you.

Each. And every one of you.

So it did. The years spoke, but we heard nothing. We sat at our tables and talked, went on standing around, at the bars, at the doors to the clubs, and we just kept talking. On and on we carried on talking about the business. Nothing had changed, really, yet everything was different.

The interior of our minds had somehow gone bust.

Opening day came, a spot of our own. The bosses, in suits bought just for the purpose, wandered among the guests. The city's assembled scenesters had gathered together, and poisonous observations made their round through little groups of movers and shakers, just as they must.

Crazy.

Suddenly the glow was snuffed out.

The goal reached.

And all at once there was no limit to the listlessness that just let the club, once achieved, go to seed. Where Wolli's always welcoming face had been that of a social world champion, now a fear of people was making its inroads.

The boss has crept off, is sitting in the back, in the offices, rolling money.

Wolli! Wake up! This can't go on. But the friendships were broken and ravaged, the marriages and lover-relationships rotted, busted, never to be redeemed.

As if to prove otherwise, an absurdly costly foreign policy was put forward. Another club had to happen, right away. A radio station is born. A new, giant spot inaugurated.

Is Wolli here? – Nah, he's upstairs. – He's not there either. – Then maybe he's on his way.

You could still see Wolli sometimes, secretly, a bottle of wine in hand, sneaking out of the back entrance of one of his own clubs, inconsolable.

Afraid of having to talk to someone.

Not wanting to listen to anything from anyone.

And not having time for anyone anymore.

All of us were: destroyed.

I had lined up a job at *Merkur*. From cowardice slightly puffed up by idealism. In a few days I had learned to bow down, under the strict supervision of my ridiculous secretary, over the highly interesting manuscripts fired off by the German professorship, the insane mental world of the budding academic council, and I was one with my miserable quest to pick out a weak or entirely absent argument from the flimsy wordplay of the dully sparkling sociology feuilletons, to dissect it, to outline and isolate it, zero to the zero power approximately, but with a speckling of cretinous adjectives. And then, on the phone with the author, I learned to ask for improved versions of unimprovably idiotic essays. Sweet gig.

I was sitting in the centre. In the heart of the spiritual heart of European thinking. In some piss-street in Glockenbach in the middle of my so detested Munich.

I ate a lot, drank a lot, I got fat and bald, dry and grey. My brain started to stink.

At night, when I couldn't sleep, I'd walk into the next room and dick around for a while with my big study, *The Lovers*. Studies about the subjects of sex, Freud, cinema. But I didn't really write the study directly, per se, instead

I looked wearily at the mountain of material before me. Material for my study of evasion, too, which was supposed to gather evidence under the title *The Süddeutsche Zeitung Has Lost Its Shit* for the prolegomenon to a projected portrait of the feuilletonist Johann Willms-Willemsen. But this study didn't write itself either, and I didn't write much of it, for that matter. Really I just sat in front of it in my repulsive stupid room. I drank wine, I drank the first bottle, and then I opened the second.

I really won't get drunk anymore somehow, I thought sometimes, anxiously. Then came the first heart attack. I thought things over, went for a cure, sat in a bathrobe in the late morning at home.

My wife: the nurse, the new boss. I love her, she thinks I'm repulsive. It's been seven years since we've slept together. Apparently she thinks I'm smart. Every day I tell her she's getting more beautiful to me every day.

Today I am also pleased to give guidance to younger writers. The collected edition of my micrograms must, as I specified in my testament years ago, appear with Suhrkamp, no exceptions, when I'm no longer here.

Corleone was a skeleton. Had become a phantom, a laughing stock. Drinking as collapse, alcoholic drinking, no fun drinking, drinking the way drinkers do: from despair, disgust, disgust at everything, at oneself. Drinking to do away with yourself.

Fucked up scene.

Very fucked up scene.

4. BOY MEETS GIRL

It's over.

I'm LYING on the ground on top of this unknown woman at Soul City, on the dance floor and the rhythm's pounding and shoving us together with ever greater brutality and I notice how insane it all is, how antisocial, how absolutely cool, and I'm about to get smacked, and she is too – and then it happens.

Ooh.

Brutal.

And we look at each other, and we're both totally smashed and sopping wet on our faces and all over, and we break out in this laughter, this crazy, bewildered and ridiculous laughter, and we roll apart. And bumping and bucking the flesh of men and women is above us, the roar of the dancing, the bump of the music, the bodies of people swaying and dancing together going in, out, coming together, pulling apart – madness, absolute madness.

Sex.

That's what is, nothing else.

That's the meaning of the whole thing here.

And we look at each other again, unknown woman and unknown man, and we see that we understand everything and we think it's totally aces and all. – And yet something else suddenly appears, a kind of shame takes over both of us, rises out of the laughter, and our eyes get bigger and take the form of a totally bizarre question – what was THAT then?! – and we both shut our eyes and hug again and lie there on the ground in the middle of the dance floor at Soul City in Munich, sweating and gasping, and we laugh, we both laugh ourselves almost half to death.

'YOU KNOW WHAT people are saying?'
  'No, to be honest, I don't know, tell me.'
People – meaning Tina Brown and Anna Wintour
– are sitting here in the dining car in the Hamburg
Königsee-Berlin Intercity saying the following, and the
following details of this little love story here, in the fol-
lowing way.
  Anna Wintour: 'But those are all internal problems
that don't matter to the reader.'
  'To our readers they do.'

IT'S TUESDAY MORNING, hour and day of
payoffs and paybacks, accusations and allegations, in-
ventions and lies and ghastly truths it would be best not
to say aloud.
  Anne says: 'Why'd you do that?'
  Steffi: 'I didn't.'
  'Eh? Come again?'
  'It's over.'
  'Over?'
  'Yeah.'
  Silence.
The phone line crackles. There's static on the lines
from Hamburg to Berlin, from Berlin to Hamburg.
Anne starts again.
  'But you knew I was with him.'
  'No, I didn't.'
  'But I told you.'
  'You told me it wasn't going anywhere.'
  'I told you I didn't know where it was going.'
  'It's going nowhere. You said that to me. You told me
he didn't even want to sleep with you anymore.'

'You're horrible.'

'You told me you were lying there and you were even naked and all of a sudden you had the feeling he thought you were disgusting. And because of that, you figured it wasn't going anywhere. That's what you said.'

Anne has started to cry.

Steffi lets the snuffling and sobbing carry on for a bit. Then starts to feel compassion for her best friend.

She gives in: 'I don't even know what you're getting so worked up about. I don't even want anything with him.'

'I don't understand.'

'I worked things out with Tim.'

'When? Why? What? How?'

'Saturday. He really is in love with me.'

'Sure. So then Monday morning you sleep with my boyfriend.'

'No. That's not how it was at all.'

'How was it then?'

'Fun. It wasn't anything serious, Anne.'

Anne exhales laboriously, shakes her head, and says: 'So you didn't actually sleep together?'

'Fuck off.'

'Please don't be obtuse: "Fuck off." What is that supposed to mean? Either you did it or you didn't.'

'I didn't.'

'So you didn't sleep with Benjamin?'

'No.'

'And you're actually willing to promise me that?'

'Yeah.'

BUT UNFORTUNATELY THIS WAS all pre-varication. There is a certain type of questioning that automatically implies a license to lie when need be. Pistol-to-the-chest type questions are forbidden

232

between best friends and lovers. And yet, in sufficiently desperate situations, these desperate questions do arise and with them the consequent lies.

Polly says again, into the silence: 'Yeah.'

Again, silence. Again, Polly: 'Seriously!'

Kevin still says nothing. And Polly can tell Kevin knows she's lying to him.

'You don't believe me anymore. That's the worst thing about all this.'

They are sitting there rather drunk, or, to be exact, super drunk, at the end of the night here at a table for two, well coked up in a swanky suite at the Hotel Renaissance in Cologne, where they're celebrating Kevin's thirty-first birthday, and at the moment they're at their wits' end, and something completely horrible is about to happen.

Kevin and Polly have been together for a good year and a half now. And for both of them, this is the one, the thing with a future, moving in together and all that. Maybe even kids, who knows. Polly has a sweet career as a midrange model, she's past twenty-six now and is starting slowly to think about what comes after. A family, maybe, one or two little roles on TV, in the movies maybe, or else she can go back to uni, study something, who knows.

She's interested in everything under the sun, especially in people. She is more the extrovert type, and at the end of the night they've partied through together, when Kevin reproaches her with the words, 'Polly, you're nothing but a big flirting machine, this is all like a joke to you,' Polly goes goggle-eyed, lifts up those heavy eyelids innocently, looks at Kevin all earnest and deep and says: 'You know me, Kevin, you know I only love you.' Then she kisses him, they sleep together, and everything's good.

They're even being faithful to each other, basically, more or less. Except for six months now Polly's been having a little *avventura* with an Italian colleague.

At some point that came to light. By now even Kevin knows out about it. They want to get through this together. They talk it over. Analyse it. They've been doing this for months now. Kevin wants to help Polly to *give up*, as they say in their innumerable conversations together, Sanjah – that's the name of Polly's Italian *inamorato*.

Talking: that is the totally unique thing about their relationship, their love. Neither of the two – they are both only children – has ever been able to talk so great with another person. That's not something you just drop at the first difficulties that arise, just because of a little Italian fling.

Polly's other little flings and affairs have fortunately not reached the stage of interrelationship-prosecution-interrogation. She worked those out on her own, talked them over with a girlfriend, in other words, somehow that worked out better.

Now with every new, still sincere conversation with Kevin, new lies come into play. Totally unintended, unavoidable lies, lies that correct the lies from before more truthfully than any truth could, and yet lies, more lies, all the same. The undergrowth keeps getting thicker, the way out less clear. The more they talk, the more mendacious the whole thing becomes. And for a long time now they've been talking, of course, about how they have to eventually stop talking about all this.

Now something's got to give.

That said, Polly naturally doesn't really want anything to give. The unfolding drama, the eternal back and forth, like in a movie, with her torn by passion, two men loving her at the same time with the same degree of intensity, she finds all that clicks with her somehow, but she can't just say that directly in front of Kevin.

She sees herself – and THIS is something she must absolutely keep secret from herself, in a way, because it would just be too ridiculous if she were to openly think this of herself – as a kind of wild volcano of wild contradictions, a highly dramatic woman of wild obsessions.

She is not the rational, calm type like Kevin. And naturally, as she explains in countless endless conversations with Hannah, she loves him for just that reason, because he *is* so full of understanding. But then on the other hand that's exactly why she obviously also can't stand him, why she adores Sanjah, but then on the other hand, the exact opposite is true too –

Polly really is just like that: winning, a bit clever, verbally very nimble, *charmante*, cheeky, almost not stupid. But sadly as it happens in the end exactly dumb enough to go on dwelling deep in the depths of the whipped up bewildered profoundly melodramatically stylized opera-emotion-world of women's magazines and to feel herself completely at home there.

A world where sexuality is conceptualized in the category and term 'good sex', which is something you 'do', and the best thing of all is 'doing it' in some exotic locale. A world, in other words, as staid, eternal, and dimwitted as Uschi Altglas or Obermeier.

This is, let us repeat, Polly's world and her future.

Kevin's long known all this. But he doesn't want to

believe it. Anything is less awful, for the moment anyway, than this: a definitive break with Polly.

But now that is the very thing that's happened. It's over. Kevin's no longer saying anything, and Polly is scared. Scared the eternal game may be suddenly and forever at an end. That at last she's overplayed her hand. That Kevin's silence is a foretaste of something horrible. And even very real, physical, brutal violence.

BENJAMIN GOES for a totally mad clean break and tells Moritz the following story.

Benjamin gets the following letter.

Dearest Steffi.

The sorrow over a broken –

Both then went into a hotel room briefly and made out there a little, and then she said:

'Come on, let's get naked!'

'Cool, yeah, good idea!'

And they took off their clothes and then they were naked and crept giggling under the thick hotel duvet and there was someone outside pounding on the door like crazy. And now the chick's best friend was there, etc. etc.

More or less immortal.

So far, so good.

SO LET'S get started and not beat around the bush. And let's do it with fifteen-year-old Mareike from Ingolstadt. She's got long brown hair, and she's into dancing, movies, reading, and music. She's looking for a guy with a sense of humour, but not too childish, and he should like techno, Quentin Tarantino, Oasis, Verve, *jetzt* magazine, maybe grunge music, like Nirvana, and he should of course not be a total idiot and maybe even understand poetry. Mareike writes poems herself and she sends us the following poem.

Jasmin talks into the camera. Then Jasmin goes to the phone in the office to talk with Johanne a moment about the latest situation.

AT THE HOTEL PHOENIX in San Francisco, Schütte sits on the king-size bed alone and talks with his girlfriend on the phone.

At the moment, Schütte is so brutally in love that he would just as soon not phone all the time. Why phone when you're on the road? A moment of control always takes hold on the phone. Something stressful always happens, you say it yourself or the other person says it, some kind of weird tone, a detail in a story, maybe a name that comes out of the blue: with total certainty something happens and in one blow it takes away all your composure.

What's the point?

Why?

Why this mutual torture?

Schütte hangs up, stands up, and starts pacing back and forth in front of the bed like a madman. Come on come on come on.

When he notices this, he stops and stands still. He shakes his head, runs his hand over his face, turns on the TV and lies down on the bed.

Schütte makes notes.

Krypse-rule. Silence everything awful.

Unfortunately though, through the silence, through this same activity of being silent, through everything that is not silence, a wedge of awfulness creeps in.

Krypse-dilemma.

What I hate so much about my girlfriend – is: I forgot.
It was so clear to me, now it's gone. Then I didn't care.
Then I forgot about it.

History of this love.

SCHÜTTE IN AMERICA. Schütte is sitting in the
New York Chinatown Holiday Inn in a gloomy broom
closet room alone on a narrow double bed reading a
fax from his girlfriend he just found on the floor as he
walked through the door, slipped, apparently through
the slit under the door.

A complaint fax, desperate. Just now, a half-hour ago,
a half a world away from here, conceived, felt, typed up,
and sent off. And this is what you get. Knowing things
that at this moment you don't want to know. Schütte's
girlfriend has taken cocaine and is now bemoaning herself, cocaine, the world, the whole nasty affair.

There's a special pleasure in reading that sort of thing.

HORRIBLE, actually, is a fitting description of almost
everything pertaining to drugs. When you're sober,
anyway. But when you yourself have taken drugs, it's
basically irrelevant. It is so hard to reconcile that in one
life, in one thought.

And so you get this anti-drug jibber jabber text, which
is nowhere to be found so far and wide as where drugs
are actually taken in large quantities. You can rant and
rave against drugs in such places, no-one's got a problem with an anti-drug brochure from the Feds.

In the past few years drugs in the scene have been getting worse and worse press all over. The cooler a person

238

feels, the more he gets riled up against drugs and drug addicts. Addiction has turned into a regular swear word, can you believe it, in the nightlife the addict is just a sorry outcast.

No joke, it's really like that.

The most pleasant, and sadly they are quite a rare breed, are those who take as many drugs as possible and criticize it as little as possible, whether it's their own use or drug use in general.

People who take few or no drugs and just drink can be totally OK, too. With drugs, as with everything else good, generally speaking, nothing is good unless you're doing it. And that's practically all there is to say.

Except for things like: You know anyone here who's got pills? I'd really love to cop a gram of cocaine. Who's pushing speed? Who's got the LSD? Where's the heroin dealer? Speaking of, heroin always sounds so heroic. OK, I'll take a little hash then, that'll be fitty.

Every fear people have about drugs is a correct fear.

Little essay concerning addiction.
    I want something
    you don't want
    that's me
    the will
    that you already are.

Schütte balled up the fax and tossed it out. Then he turned on the TV.

Monday Night Football.

Still: they are all here, the stories, the dreams, the inspirations.

5. CLUB CANOSSA

'Parrrty Parrrty, Parrrty.'

HI RAVER! The summer is drawing to an end, autumn has thrown on its colourful robes. Time to enjoy the last open-air summer chill-out: caipirinha, midday sun, joint.

But for later, we've cooked up a few superb stimulations for all those who might not have had enough fun. Once again, our motto this time, how lovely, is this: 'Faster, higher, longer, deeper.' Anyone who hasn't signed up yet should do so now at the latest.

And so: do as much cocaine as possible.

Keep going as long as you can.

Get hold of more cocaine.

Take cocaine.

And more.

More, I said.

MORE.

So what was the question again? Right, could you lend me 200 marks real quick, or 400 maybe? Please! I said. And make it snappy.

I. THY WILL BE DONE

For tonight now we may tentatively have got just a little bit coked up here, coked up and coked out for the time being, easy does it.

Schütte, Tiermann, a John Doe, Brother No Limits, him, and me.

Who's cutting it up?

This dude, that dude.
Anything to say?
What for?
Just in case.
Not really. Not that I can think of.
Good.

Pause.

Maybe we'll have one more, a nice little discreet one,
what do you think?
   Absolutely.
   For sure. – Yep.
   In.

Something totally new: a pause.
   A pause when nothing is said, nothing happens.
   And really: nothing at all.

Then more cocaine gets snorted.
   People nod and sit back down.
   Agreeable calm, nothing hectic.
   A few stressful thoughts, in part.
   What kind of thoughts?
   Nothing important, nothing worth sharing.
   Got it.

Calm.

Maybe another line, nice and easy?
   Why not?
   Someone cuts it up.
   Real calm everyone gathers round.
   Then sits back down and nods pleasantly.

Time passes.

Paranoia.
    Have I gone too long without saying anything?
    Is the mood altogether OK?
    Would the others rather be alone?
    Am I being too polite? So polite that it's annoying?
    Too impolite?
    What kind of fucked up dude am I, mentally
speaking?
    Pretty fucked up.
    Could that be getting on the others' nerves?
    Tough situation.
    Would...?
    What do I do?

    Who's cutting?
    Someone cuts, then everyone snorts again.
    Real nice, thanks.
    What do you mean, *thanks?*
    Dimwit.
    Tear paper from the roll lying on the table and clean
out your so-called nose a little. So you can get a little
something into it.
    Your mucous membranes are still offering some
slight resistance.

pff

Something was
    what was?
    yee
    empty too

Pause – Silence – Calm
  Text-standstill.

Confrontation with the ego structure, which –
  eh, what

new call
  sure
  yeah yeah
  bitter pill – right number

explain then – explained – nah now
  how come?
  best not –
  OK

Tell me then
  the situation we've got into here –
  right then

thingy

eh

another?
  absolutely
  how did you know just the thing to say?
  maybe we should all snort a bit more cocaine
  nice deep breath: fff fff fffff
  hm
  that goes down good

AGITATION
  the most brutal agitation

the most brutal agitation
extremely cool

still?
    def

little more?
    for sure

Thus a beautiful long summer comes to an end.

II. SHAKEN SHACK

'The language transport will last a little bit longer.'

... and a woman, Schütte scribbles half-asleep on a piece
of paper, that –
    who...–
    He sinks back.
    He sleeps.

Woody 24/7. Motte nonstop.
    The music hasn't stopped even once on the day after
the nightly night. People are even talking about mellowness now, about a gentleness of mood, the close-up
perspective of a harmonic spirit strange to them at first.
    It emerges from the bodies of the sleeping, played
softly by two loudspeakers, returns inside them to find
resonance deep in the interior of their living essence.
    A cat walks through the room, meows in Marc's face,
then walks on and snuggles against Woody's leg. Woody
runs one hand over its fur while with the other he flips
calmly through a stack of records.

He smokes, and his eyes wander around the room.

Once upon a time, there were not yet words for all this here. It just happened, and you were in the midst of it, you watched and had some kind of thoughts, but no words.

Does that even exist? Maybe only inside, in the mind?

Sure, always.

It was the wordless time, when we were always looking around with our big eyes so strangely in every possible situation, shaking our heads, and could almost never say anything but:

speechless –

pf –

brutal –

madness –

speechless, really –

That was our ode to happiness. What we were expressing was astonishment, awe before the overwhelming, the stunning, the simple and unspectacular and yet somehow monumental quality of the moments we inhabited, which permeated us; an expression of the feeling that we had never experienced and couldn't imagine anything cooler and more dope etc etc.

Great wonder then, great bafflement.

Where am I, what was that?

Hm?

The situation afterwards: uff.

And there, when nobody yet knew for certain what all that really meant, what arose above all was the need to repeat it. To repeat it again and again. I don't know exactly how long this lasted, it was so one with you that it was impossible to remember.

Beautiful, super-beautiful – but also deficitary. It lacked something. And in everyone, one way or another, this inner thing was being worked at.

Around and inside you, you have the progenitor, its name is language, and it begins quite simply with 'Sh shsh... – ' But then it breaks off and crashes and rumbles and rattles: The 'bb –' bursting language, pronounced, an 'eh... – .' Astonishment in the eyes, a nodding, a yes. Yes, I – . What now! it hisses back, incensed, vengeful, with its brutal: 'ch! chch!' What then? The words, the cawings, the crushers that let themselves be made into makers, thrown out into the world, yellow, poison yellow of the 'e.' Understand, understand. – Understand: the conclusion of language I understand poorly. Maybe change places with the words and eventually be somewhere else through understanding?

Who cares?

In reality though, it was different. Or at least it was different at the same time. We didn't speak only with words broken up and pulled out of us, we just talked, more or less simply, the way people just talk, just told each other what was, what had happened, what was popping off.

For example, Christmas, when we drank these Austrian slimming drops, and me and Woody wandered through the Christmas passers-by zone looking for a quiet place to roll one up.

Or way before that, with Hell and Steve, after the Omen, one of the very first Omen Nights. We sat there wasted the morning after on the sunning balcony on the Körnerwiese and we just went on with everything because everything was still going on and the music emerged softly from the room where the others were sleeping and so we sat there in the mild glow of the early summer morning sun for hours, endlessly, and talked and talked.

Or something like that. That's how the stories always went everywhere, no?

And later we were sitting one afternoon at Two Sisters with Martina, and Virginia and Sassy were telling Anki exactly how things had gone after the scene at the bar in Far Fugo. Every Monday and Tuesday the burnouts would sit around somewhere in little groups like that and tell each other what they'd done and been through the whole weekend long.

Reckless as it might have been, at the same time this experience was yearning to understand itself. And yet wanting at the same moment to forget itself again, to destroy understanding, to have some new experience reveal that understanding to be nonsense invalidated through novelty, tumult, coolness.

In the beginning were the words. The words consisted of repetitions of words newly born in the nightlife. There was a time when you could actually get the best sense of what was going on by checking out the comics in *Groove* and reading the sayings Zille had captured in them. Inevitably you said: That's true, they said, we said, something just like that. And so it was.

The narratives reiterated the external data, too, names and places, times and movements, the pure passing of events. And over time, the sound of these stories started to have something novel to it, something minimal but not entirely inaudible. It was in writing that I heard for the first time about Eve & Rave, when we were looking at this little party drug booklet at the Partysan offices in the attic. Hey, what's that? Someone's finally found the tone. But who wrote it?

The language was different. In the interior of the body, the music, the dancing, the endless hours of doing more and more and the never going home and taken all together the extreme unstoppable nature of the thing, had altered at once the space of resonance in each individual, and at the same time the collective space where language sways back and forth, to test whether language even halfway conveys everything thought and intended.

You cannot imagine to a sufficient degree the breadth of this oscillation Soul Brain raised to Word through Heart. Probably Saturn is the distant heavenly body responsible. That's why everything lasts so long, and melancholy casts its strange shadow over it.

So like now Woody was sitting there like so and smoking, and neither the cat nor the spirit of the moment, neither the music playing nor the records flipped through, neither the sleepers lying piled up on and around the mattress on the floor nor even he himself were truly the object and centre of his instantaneous attention, instead it was all of that together, in a certain way –

Again this was a moment when this special extreme was fleetingly the truth:

that everything is there in everyone,

that everyone knows everything,

and that sometimes you sense this and on the rarest occasions notice how it is outwardly expressed in eternally unexpected ways. And that for just this reason alone strife is wrong, because it forgets all this, and that the life of destruction we lead is a gift, and is right in spite of everything.

I couldn't see which record Woody chose in that instant and put on.

I lay there and slept and had the feeling that Basic Channel's *Ninth* was playing inside me.

III. BOOK OF SOBRIETY

'I'd have had something to say about that, too.'

When we woke up, we felt fresh and we took speed and rolled one up. I read *Liquid Sky Echo*, which Claudia had just fetched just for me out of the car, the poems and the *Sexy Test* and I laughed myself silly.

Kiss?
Know?
Remember?
Are you on drugs?
Nah, I'm just on drugs.
Wolfgang and I huff some Pattex.
Twelve kolsches and three grams of coke.

Dis (solution).

Slowly this plan came together to drive to the Teenie Showcase at Park Café. Mr President was playing there that day. Cool plan, just a little bit hard to carry out. In our collective circumstances it was almost impossible to become collectively capable of action. Everyone still had to do, deal with, say, dispatch, take, set up, organize, phone up, or assemble, until a departure could finally be organized.

So we finally make it over there and Mr President is already in the encore playing their biggest hit, 'We're flying high'. A makeshift stage is set up in front of the DJ pulpit and the squealing kids and kiddies crowd in front of it. The appearance is clearly a success. New image, new record company, Consti explains. All involved are feeling optimistic.

At the bar Martin Pesch, Tim Renner, and Moritz von Oswald stand there and clap. The encore is over, and Mr President has stiffened into a motionless three-piece sculpture. On the two edges of the stage are the two so-called sexy dancers, in garters, doing splits, and frozen like the rest of them. Then the lights go off and on, and Mr President takes a bow, first the three of them, then the five, and when they start applauding the public in turn, the jubilation hits a high note. Not bad.

The A&R overseeing German dance for the new record label Motor socks Hans Jürgen Krahl, the mastermind and producer of Mr President, on the shoulder, and says:

'Mr Krahl, this is going places. I'm glad!'

And he utters this 'I'm glad' in the manner of a quote, the way Harald Schmidt does when he quotes Patti Lindner saying 'I'm glad.' Then Renner and Krahl toast and they really are glad.

'What do you say, Mr Pesch?' Renner says to Pesch, though they've known each other for years and the Mr isn't really necessary. Martin Pesch is chief reporter for *Bravo* and oversees the whole *Dance* section, German as well as international, and he's got a pretty good idea of how this story here is going to go. He wants to approach it pretty much the same way as he did the Mouse on Mars story, which got a good bit of international acclaim: music that makes you ask questions. That even gives the ear new tasks, sometimes, when the flowing beat breaks.

Twelve-year-old girls are particularly receptive to these poetic, existential tones, as the letters to the editor prove. Even with the Mr President story he wants to foreground the broken, the questionable. And he says now to Renner: 'In a better world, that would be a hit. Ha! With this line-up. That's going to catch on, I'll bet on that.'

At *Bravo* Martin Pesch sees himself as a sort of '90s version of Neil Tennant, but less subversive than the latter was in his day. Pop today is ten times bigger in all directions than it was then: cleverer, cooler, more screwed up, richer, more complex and whatnot. Martin Pesch now addresses the chick with critical interests who pounces on him because he was going to sell out to *Bravo* or else already had.

Not at all, Martin Pesch explained, this is about a totally new understanding of music, politics, and press, about the bandwidth that runs from the most standardized twisted electro-experiments for the average *House Attack* reader to the standardized predictable *Club Rotation* sound, which the *Spex* readership has slowly started grooving to in the past couple of years.

What are they talking about now?

We were standing directly next to them at the bar and our thing was so different that all this sounded to us in essence like pure lunacy and nonsense. But even this was all probably also true in some way. There was just one thing that definitely wasn't: that words are the only conceivable and real form of intelligence, and those who produce words are automatically intelligent. Quite the opposite, in fact.

Maybe it was also a question of sobriety, hence of the momentary circumstance, of Tuesdays in general, if you will. Because everywhere, in every office connected to the nightlife, in the record companies and editors' rooms, in the promoters' agencies and designers' agencies, Tuesdays are when sober people get the floor. Quite automatically, because the people fucked up from partying were still too fucked up to show up to work, some were still lost in some private after-hours somewhere, still out of commission, like us today.

Always, always on Tuesdays, time, the years have imposed on the whole nightlife get-up a rather strange, quite alien, brief interlude of conventionality, a dim-wit-selection that probably in the end was what made *Front Page* get played out and go belly-up, probably it was that more than the megalomaniacal conceptual lunacy of their visionary-crackpot founder JL, etc. etc.

And finally driving over to P1 again, where there was no Blub Club today, anyway. On this normal Tuesday P1 almost completely empty.

This, then, is the other kind of perfect day at P1, the day when no-one is there except P1, the absolute club, itself. The epitome, the constant, the very definition of the institution: THE club. Bigger than anything any bigwig could ever think of. The definition of Munich, as the dear Lord God resolved at some point: FC Bayern, Hofbräuhaus, Oktoberfest, P1. And whenever we hear anything anywhere about these four Munich house brands, we Munichers can rejoice that they are from Munich. For us, at least, this is joy.

Wolli, who's working Tuesdays alone at the back bar, is squatting in the shadowy niche and writing things to do in his notebook.

What he has to do tomorrow.

Who he will say what to tomorrow.

Calculations. Projects. Ideas.

Often you can find me there too, around twelve: I order a non-alcoholic beer and we smoke a Lucky or an HB and talk about what's new, what's newest. What's newest today: all at once, today, I've got a clear sense about how this little booklet here might progress, maybe. And so I tell Wolli right away, fresh, amped up, all that.

The story with the dark core and the wicked hero, with the hermetically sealed plot, the time-structure of absolute presence, and how cool that's all going to be.

What do you think, Wolli?

IV. AESTHETIC THEORY

'My pussy is as pretty as a rose.'

'Monday didn't do it for me.'

The *jetzt* diary issue has come out again.

I'm lying in bed.

I'm reading *jetzt* and Keith Haring's Diaries.

Love: in the story of a young woman, straight-up love madness, which brings together the tenderness and hardness, the ruthlessness and the gentleness of her nature.

There was no more fear of going insane, because it had become reality.

So that was inside all of us.

Diary. Tuesday. You must wrest language free from its communicative intention. Writing as nothing more than autistic, pure scribbling dictated by time itself – breath. Beyond death. But it must await the advent of the latter in order to become text.

How sad.

Schütte is lying in the bathtub.

And the silence now is absolutely grandiose.

It's the first time in countless hours and many days that he's totally alone. Hot water, element of elements, surrounds him, and in his totally hollow head a downy emptiness, how you come to recognize it, nameless things, moments, and in their midst a few images, tatters, and scenes. Sentences, quotes, moments.

A weekend.

Already.

For they know not what they do.

Who does even.

Let him first cast a stone.

I would even go on the Harald Schmidt Show, sure, but only if I don't have to do or say anything. I imagine Harald Schmidt has explained in many interviews the fundamental principles, so to speak, of his guest treatment policy, all his thoughts concerning it and how it actually goes in practice, and that everything would furthermore be explicitly explained and laid out for me. You've just got to do it so well that practically nothing comes up, that I don't say anything, that just he talks. The effect of that isn't some perverse avoidance, is actually pleasant for the viewer, normally, on practically every episode, the torture begins as soon as the guests come onstage. I explain all this to the editor on the phone. And Harald Schmidt in the end would talk about LANGUAGE. And I would explain a few things to him beforehand, things he doesn't totally get, about the difference between English, American, and German, things I had Jay Leno say in the *Interview* cover story. And Harald Schmidt would then explain the things I had explained to him and so on and so forth. I don't know, I imagine it as fucking funny, but funny in a different way from us wriggling around all sexy with one another, as soon as that starts, I get a genital spasm and I have to change channels. Like before with Gottschalk and the Polish miracle boobs. The miracle bookworm. Dudes who write books, a type everyone thinks is cool who always just says yes and is in total agreement with everything, and then he writes these bizarre, tedious books. A certain concept of reality, a media idea, a way of watching TV. The artificiality of aspect: appearance. How all that functions. The kind of knowledge-machine that is constantly running there, what a truly unbelievable personal-revelation-mechanism the TV is. Done. Short and sweet. Bye now, till next time, thanks. And in two and a half, three minutes all I would have said was: YES EXACTLY, yeah, yeah. But from the depths of my heart, because Harald Schmidt would have spoken to me from the heart. That would be cool, right.

Language: no.
　　Yes: a concrete life.

I note down how Hardy told me at the Sonic Empire Platinum Awards, in the inner courtyard of the Kehr Wieder Bar where the event took place, that I had stayed away from the studio to note something down. And this was just when they had finished listening to the final version of 'Hard Times', and Westbam said to him – and when he told me this, he did so in Westbam's voice:

'So, my Hardy, what do you have to say about this piece?'

And Hardy said he said: 'I'll give it a devout pause of the strobes.'

And I was talking later with Katrinchen and she said: 'I can capitalize on that until the cows come home!' – And I asked: 'Can I write that down real quick?' – And she laughed and said: 'Of course.'

Then: crazy dreams, tons, recently about Mate, who said the year to come had to be extremely 'kippy', after last year – and we didn't really know what that meant.

While cleaning: acts of feeblemindedness and melancholy.

Diaries. I just can't read enough of them. Every other life is so interesting, in its view of itself, the more interesting, the stranger it is.

Keith Haring: dead.

Hubert Fichte: dead.

Andy Warhol: dead.

But with Ernst Jünger, Helmut Krausser, and Peter Rühmkorf, who are all still alive, the effect remains consistently incredible: you get sucked in, pulled ineluctably inside, and at the same time drawn so terribly away. Just like with real life. And it makes a person no less sad. Diaries do you in. Like the TV last night at 10.32 p.m.:

Valediction and death

are everpresent there,

but so is love.

But at the same time a music that –

takes you away from it, from the music, and from yourself. That takes you away from thinking, from attentiveness, from the precision of retracing the distinctly conceived individual steps of thought, from reflection in the sense of recalling successions of thoughts. Which exempts all others' collective vote of life and even the living cells that keep the cerebral cortex alive from the absolutism of inevitably exclusively discrete thinking, which the cerebral cortex can only grasp in discrete terms at a discretely defined moment, not to abrogate the absolutist thinking structure, but to complement it, as it were.

A kind of biological surplus of intake normally to be found in the nightlife through dancing, the grandiose violence of clamour, and drugs: a perfect translation of all that into music, so the effect is still there when you're home alone listening with the volume down: that is what Basic Channel accomplishes.

A monotony that actually speaks the language of living, and therefore, however externally minimal it appears, actually generates a maximum of fundamentality and depth. For many this takes root so deep inside the body that it brings a spiritual element into play. Well, then. The body is an unfathomable sanctuary infinitely distant from nomenclature and epistemological manoeuvres.

Maurizio
Basic Channel
Main Street Records
Burial Mix

And then, in a kind of secondary, often even more fascinating reflection on these base elements, lots of Chain Reactions. It's hard for me to really grasp how a couple of people in Berlin were capable, in the Hardwax and Dubplate and Mastering climate, to penetrate so deep and so effortlessly into the hyper-individual. Where did they get that from? How did they manage to break out? An absolute riddle.

Every new record you come across is so individually beautiful, like a new artwork by On Kawara. Monumental real Buddhism. Wisdom and courage. Political vision: the same in everything.

The mountains.

The sea.

A few stones somewhere.

The thought of Joseph Beuys.

Art you don't see. Music you don't hear. A thought that has already dispensed with everything thinkable and thus gives everyone total freedom and leaves you so simply completely in peace. Complete.

The secret of concealment

Nonoversignificance

Flow

Doris

Franziska

Silvia

I don't know them all. Only Doris.

Could you please take out all the value judgements, please?

– sure, no problem

– this one too, please

– like this?

– yes, that's better

– no problem

– thank you so much
– you are certainly most welcome.

Fuzzy ordering of concepts.
    Scattered thought amid dopamine-schizophrenia.
    I am exactly as far from the two dead siblings as from the two living ones.
    I stand in the very middle.

broadly diffuse arousal

V. THE NOVICE

'We'll never stop living this way.'

You must say it three times, Lord.

We followed a dark interior voiceless compulsion that said: Stand up and go.
    Where to, Lord?
    Out.

We are sitting there still and now we will go.

I'm sitting alone on a bench in the Kantstrasse, in a garden on Savignyplatz, and looking at the magazine in front of me: *Artforum*, Jeff Koons cover story. I know I am brutally interested in it, but I feel absolutely NOTHING of this interest. I read the words in the article and take a look at the pictures. What all of it tells me is absolutely NOTHING. This total non-effect fascinates me, the gelid nonresponse inside me.
    Anyone home? – Nope. – Cool.

A giant hollow cathedral of emptiness, where in the corners, perhaps, a few platitudes still hang around hollow, filed smooth.

The giiiirl again. Never too much. Eh? Maybe, yeah, actually, as much as possible, too much if possible, too much. What say you?

We take off and walk to the exhibition opening in the so-called academy. The fine arts. Someone's giving a speech, jam packed.

We meet in the bathroom.

Way better.

The corners of the mouth tug down, the mood up.

No panic now.

Better if we go out for a bit.

Not uncomplicated to master, this thing.

Pity.

My head.

Maybe it's a test of character of some kind, a sort of study against myself, a character study? Hard.

I would gladly explain a great deal, but it is not at all clear to me whether at this moment that would not stray too much into intimate details.

Disturbing.

How powerfully synchronous or asynchronous is a person ticking at any given moment?

So we go wandering through Tiergarten. The paths up and down, back and forth.

Playgrounds, lone benches.

Phone booths.

Yeah: those are places for us, where we can go about

our business.

Then go again, quick, steady.

That feels good now.

I sit alone in the gutter somewhere, between parked cars, try to ingest. People keep coming, I feel like I'm being watched. Twitching in the knees, the card, the hand. Pathetic. We all need a bit more practice with this. I'm still a little too spacy to go home.

We've been here before, at this crossing. It seems familiar to me. You too?

We sit on a bench, we've lost the phone card. It happens.

Endless taxi ride.

Up to now I had never quite properly grasped that I live in the middle of fucking nowhere.

Finally home, in peace.

Better to just dose than to dose for some effect.

There's a little something left.

Very nice.

Naturally got to get rid of this. Now.

Exactly.

The TV's on.

For the novice: the social act is in a minor crisis.

Just for now maybe? What's wrong? There's something that doesn't quite work.

You don't know what. How come?

I can't follow the action on the TV.

The hours glower.

The burnout: now paralysis.
Disquiet.
Inner torment.
Knowledge that at least you're doing the right thing:
participating. Participating: lovely.

What is fading
fades.
Earth
to earth.
Ashes to ashes.
Dust
to dust.

We dodder out. At the very end of our rope, we walk
along the pavement. Unbelievable, we pull ourselves to-
gether. We've let ourselves go to shit. We didn't expect
we'd ever get the bill for all that. We turn the entire ar-
mada of our inner strength against disappointment.
That's not nothing.
It works.
We find a taxi.
A moment of great proximity, in wordless misery.
Gratitude.
Our friend gets into the taxi and says the famous last
words by way of goodbye.

And later we tell ourselves how this moment was, which
restored to us in our hour of need and devastation a last
vestige of dignity, yes. No, we won't stop living this way.